Congratulations on you ... [barcode M000033639]

Oak, what you have here with *A Man True* is a simple, straightforward story but with beautiful Christian themes chosen with care. Your portrayal of the setting is good; we are given a strong sense of the era from the details, and your description of good old-fashioned manners and chivalry makes one yearn for the good old days. The main characters set such a charming example in holy conduct, it's easy to see how this would be great book for the shelves of every conscientious Christian family that understands the importance of raising and training a child "in the way he should go" (Prov. 22:6).

—Editor's Note

Numbers 6:24-2...

A MAN
TRUE

Timothy W. Bryant

A MAN
TRUE

REDEMPTION
PRESS

Published by Redemption Press, PO Box 427, Enumclaw, WA 98022

Toll Free (844) 2REDEEM (273-3336)

Redemption Press is honored to present this title in partnership with the author. The views expressed or implied in this work are those of the author. Redemption Press provides our imprint seal representing design excellence, creative content, and high quality production.

ISBN: 978-1-68314-288-1

Library of Congress Catalog Card Number: 2017934502

To my wife,

FAITH.

Your love has always made me want to be a better man.

Contents

1

Eli

The baby was warm against my chest, and seemed content to sleep wrapped snugly to me with a sling I had seen Cherokee Indian mothers use. Under my long wool coat with its heavy cape, at first glance someone might not notice the child, but they would notice the Henry rifle, with its two-foot-long octagon barrel and sixteen-shot magazine and brass receiver, slung across my back. With too close of a look, they might also notice the two Remington Army .44-caliber handguns with extra-loaded cylinders, one for each. Just a little too close, there would be a twelve-inch-long, two-inch-wide-bladed Bowie knife. Not an easy weapon to ignore.

These weapons, this long heavy wool coat, a pair of boots, and Momma's Bible were left for me in a large wooden box at the army headquarters in Memphis. When I stepped off the paddleboat from New Orleans, there was a young army private there to meet me. He seemed to recognize me, said if I were to follow him there were arrangements made for me to stay. When I entered my quarters, there was this large crate in the middle of the room. In the box, a note read, "Thought you might need these for the journey and Momma's Bible for the new job. William."

There would be no harm come on this child while I have a bullet or an ounce of strength left in my body. A strong body has run in my family for many generations. Broad shoulders, hands larger than most, and just enough love of a good fight when put upon to convince men they have made a mistake of laying a hand on me.

Besides, this child has suffered enough, what with the loss of her dad and most likely her mother, unless my doctorin' helps her heal and I can manage a warm dry place for us to hole up. No sir, those men may stay on my back trail and they may even catch us, but this child is safe.

Recalling the events of the previous night seemed to help take my mind off the lack of sleep, plus the load I carried: baby Emma, weapons, and supplies for the three of us. Then there was keeping an eye on Mercedes as she struggled to stay on the horse. Now I walked beside the horse with my hand on a belt around her waist after she came too close to falling to the ground.

Just on the Arkansas side of the Mississippi, an hour or so after dark, I came upon the camp. The screaming put me and the dogs to caution, moving slowly in the dark up to the edge of the camp, keeping myself and the horse back in the dark just enough to see into the camp but not be seen or heard. Easing out of the saddle, both dogs moved close to me, sensing the danger, ears up waiting and watching with me. By count, there were a dozen men in the camp, a large covered wagon, and one man tied to one of the wagon wheels. Appeared I would be there too late for him, but the woman on the ground slowly rose to her feet. Twelve men by my count, not a one reached out to help her up. The fire and rage began to come on me; there were only twelve by my count. On her feet, she faced the largest of the twelve and the one who seemed to be giving the orders. A big man, even by my standards.

She was tall for a woman, hair and eyes dark. Even with what I believe the big man had put her through before I arrived, she looked strong. "Sign the papers," the big man said to her. "I will take the child and let you live." Slowly she turned to the wagon. From the wagon, a baby began to cry.

So quickly, she turned on the big man, the slap sounded like a gunshot setting him back on his heels. Then she was on him. The next scream was his as her fingers dug into his eyes, her momentum took him to the ground. His head made a *crack* sound as it hit a rather large rock next to the fire. Then there was a shot, smoke came from around the woman's waist. She lay on top of him, and neither was moving. That was the moment I decided to enter the camp.

Now the horse I had been riding was a bit skittish, so my first shot sent him on a wild run straight through the camp and dead set on running over the fella holding the reins to their horses. Trampled by my horse, he lets go of the horses and they all take off into the dark with my horse. The rest of the men didn't notice me at first, with the lady taking out their leader and my horse running through the camp. I moved just into the edge of the campfire light and purposely shot the first two men low in the legs. Thumbing the hammers back on those two Remington Army .44 calibers, I took two more men out, one in the shoulder, another low and in the legs. Killing would be easy, and these men seemed deserving of killing, but I had seen too much death in the war. Running through the smoke from my shots, I struck hard across the head of the next man with the octagon barrel of one of the Remingtons. He went down and out. That left six men bunched together facing me, the sound of me pulling the hammers back on those two pistols, and the dogs' teeth bared. Low growling caused four of them to decide to leave in a hurry. Scared men running always seems to cause dogs to give chase. The other two dropped their guns but did not seem ready to leave.

"Mister, you don't know whose business you are gittin' into or you would leave now. Those men that left will be back, and there's gonna be more with them."

I had nothing to say to these men at this point. Keeping my guns on them, I moved to the wagon. Looking in the back, I could see a small child wrapped in a blanket. The tailgate was down on the wagon. I still had nothing to say, but I laid both pistols down on the tailgate. With a prayer under my breath, I said, "Lord, please help me not to kill these men." What kind of men would treat a woman and child like this? The rage in me was almost more than I could bear. After the war, the guilt of the killing was—is—so heavy on my soul. I wished no harm on no one. But a child, a woman, treated with such disrespect had to be answered hard.

Two quick steps and I was face-to-face with the two men. I kicked their weapons away. The one who had spoken had a knife carried low in his right hand and lunged straight at me, thrusting upward as he came in. Leaning back just enough for the knife to miss, I grasped his wrist with my left hand, pulling him into my right fist. At that moment, the other man to my left swung a fist to my side; the pain of the blow did not keep me from breaking the man's wrist as I yanked him into the other man. The scream and the sound of bones breaking gave the second man no chance to avoid a blow on the chin, a blow that I set my feet for and swung from the waist. They would both be out for a while.

The baby began to cry, so I stepped to the back of the wagon, quickly holstered my two guns, reached into the wagon and pulled out a large basket. The baby was wrapped snugly but was very unhappy. So I lifted the baby gently out—a girl, I believe, because of the lace and very small pink bonnet on her head. Even with the blanket wrapped around her, she barely filled my two large hands. Picking her up calmed her, and then there was a sound behind us. It was her mother. Carrying the child, I went to her. She had rolled onto her back, alive but shot low on her left side. The big man was holding a pistol when she had attacked him. Looking at him, I could see the right eye was bad; a lot of blood from the eye and the crack on his head. He was of no concern to me now; she was, and I knew the bleeding had to be stopped.

Her eyes seemed so dark. Seeing the baby and me holding the child, I could see the fear in her, fear for her baby in the hands of this large, unshaven, weathered man. For all she knew, I was one of them. So I gently unwrapped the blanket and laid the baby on her chest, and then covered them both with the blanket. The next thing I did was something I learned from my mother and father. I laid both of my large hands on them, eyes closed, head bowed, and began to pray.

"Lord, hear my prayer, have mercy on these two ladies. I don't know what has brought us together, but I believe you had a hand in it, so I ask for your strength and healing and your peace. Also, Lord, forgive me the hurt I put on those men. You know they deserved it. Amen."

When I opened my eyes, the fear in hers had gone, and she whispered, "The baby's name is Emma."

The dogs were back. Mary-Lou had blood around her mouth and Bill had a boot in his, which he dropped at my feet. Then both dogs moved slowly to the lady and baby, gently putting their noses against them, making a soft whimpering sound. They both sat back on their haunches and looked at me. "Good dogs. We are going to take care of these ladies."

"Friends?"

"Yes, ma'am, they are."

"Sir?"

"Yes, ma'am?"

"May I have your name, please?"

"Elijah, Elijah Johnson."

"Sir."

"Yes, ma'am?"

"There is milk and clothes for Emma in the wagon. Please see after my baby girl."

"Call me Eli, ma'am. She is safe with me. You both are. Let me see to your wound, then I will add supplies from the wagon to my supplies, for you and Emma, and we need to move. I believe those men will be back, and some of these men lying around will start coming to soon."

There was a nudge on my left; it was Mary-Lou. She had dragged the basket over for the baby, so gently

Eli

I lifted Emma from her mother's chest, laid her in the basket, and covered her. Both dogs moved to either side of the basket. At this point there would be a problem touching the basket or its contents without their permission.

I turned to the lady to care for her wound. Her dress was a dark blue with large buttons down the front to the waist. "Ma'am, may I have your name?"

"Mercedes," she whispered low, eyes barely open.

"Mercedes, I will have to open the front of your dress to care for your wound, is that okay?"

Then suddenly with both hands she grabbed my coat and pulled herself up to me, her eyes black and wide open. "Eli, they will be back and they want my baby."

The terror in her eyes went away only because she passed out. Quickly I dressed her wound; the bullet went clean through, but it tore a large hole going in and coming out. She was losing a lot of blood fast; a tight field dressing with some packing, and both wounds and the bleeding slowed. After we left and I found us a safe place to stop, I would dress the wound again. The army had taught me how to kill, but also how take care of a wound in the field.

Going through the wagon, I found a ladies' bag with baby clothes, also cans of evaporated milk for the baby, some blankets, and food: coffee, some bacon, and dried fruit to add to my supplies. A leather pouch lay under her bag; inside, it had some papers that looked important, so I stuffed it into the large bag with the baby supplies. I had dropped my saddlebags off the horse before entering the camp. Good thing, 'cause I don't think he will be coming back. Returning to camp after fetching my saddlebags, there stood Bill with the reins of one of their horses in his mouth, and let me tell ya, it was a beauty. Blackest horse I ever saw with a small blaze and two white front stockings. Mary-Lou, on the other hand, had not left the side of baby Emma and mother.

Eli

I had our supplies loaded on the horse when I turned to see Mercedes standing. Two quick steps and I had her in my arms before she fell, then I lifted her onto the saddle. The horse seemed very gentle, as if he knew her and knew she was not well. Taking Emma, we headed into the darkness; by the moon and stars, I believed it to be about midnight.

The horse stumbled, or I did, causing Mercedes to tense up and release a small moan. I believe that man had broken one or two of her ribs; if he survived his injuries and I should ever cross paths with him, God help me.

We had been traveling twenty-four hours, only stopping to feed the baby and give Mercedes a break. She refused to eat, only drank some water, ever asking about Emma, drifting in and out of consciousness. I knew I had to find shelter soon, someplace where we could hole up for a while so I could get some food in her and she might sleep.

In the last few miles, we had left the flat country and were now in the Ozarks of Arkansas. I had been heading to this country before I involved myself with these ladies. I believe by daylight we should be at a settlement called Newport on a large bend in the White River. There, maybe I can find a place for the ladies to stay.

Suddenly, Mercedes began to shake. I quickly reached my right arm up around her; she fell over on my shoulder as I lifted her from the horse. We would have to stop.

Just ahead, with the moonlight, I could see a large outcropping of rocks. Not more than thirty yards ahead, there loomed in the darkness a large rock overhang. I walked under the large rock with Mercedes over my shoulder, and saw that it opened back about forty feet. I carried her to the back of the overhang, laid her gently down—not easy with Emma still wrapped to me. Once she was laid down on what felt in the darkness to be very thick moss, I unwrapped Emma from my chest and laid her beside Mercedes. The dogs moved in close and lay beside them. That black horse had followed us and stood just at the edge of the overhang where he had found some grass; which was good, because my bacon and coffee were in the saddlebags on him.

I found some large rocks and stacked them in a way around a small hole I dug for the fire to be reflected back into the cave. There was plenty of dry wood, and soon I had a fire going and extra wood close by.

After pulling the saddle from the horse, I laid it on the ground besides Mercedes, covered it with the saddle blanket, then slowly and gently laid her head on the saddle. When I removed the dressing from her wound, it began to slowly bleed. Quickly I cleaned the wound with water and remembered a paste made of honey given to me by a doctor I had made friends with in England. Taking it from my saddlebag, I applied it to the wound, then wrapped it with a clean cloth.

With the fire going, I had water heating in my small coffeepot. I shaved some salted beef jerky into a cup and poured the hot water over it, making a beef broth. As I turned from the fire to Mercedes, she was looking at me but was not sure who I was. She said, "Please help my baby, sir."

"Yes, ma'am," said I. "Ms. Emma is fine. I am taking good care of her. You need to drink this, ma'am." As I put the broth to her lips, she took a little, swallowed slowly, then took some more. Little by little, I was able to get two cups of my broth down her, then she turned her head to one side and went to sleep. Now for the baby; she had been very quiet, so I wondered if she was okay. I checked the bag in the wagon and found diapers and a bottle. The bottle was very welcome as I was not sure how to git the milk in her otherwise; 'course on the trail, her mother had been feeding her mother's milk. She proved to have a good appetite, which made me believe she was healthy. And did she like to smile.

The canned milk I watered down, just as I had seen my wife do for our child.

There was frost on the fallen leaves, normal for middle of March. I stepped from the cave at dawn; both dogs ran past me down to the creek below the cave. The horse I had tied to a tree was just under the overhang at the cave entrance. I untied the horse and we walked down to the creek to join Bill and Mary-Lou for a drink and to get some fresh water for coffee. We should leave soon, but Mercedes had a fever in the night, just as the night before.

Upon my return to the cave I found both ladies asleep, so I stirred the coals of the fire, added some wood, then sat the coffeepot to boil. Once boiling, I sprinkled a few drops of cold water in the pot to settle the grounds, and had my first cup, always the best.

Stepping to the edge of the cave entrance looking down toward the creek, I found a large flat rock to sit on and watch the dogs run up and down the creek. The horse I had left on a small patch of grass by the creek;

he seemed content there. The dogs noticed me, heads up as soon as I appeared from the cave, watched me a minute to see if I would call or motion for them to come. When I did not, they returned to exploring the creek for food. Thinking of our situation, I knew we would have to leave no later than tomorrow; we would be out of supplies and milk for the baby. Mercedes had fed the baby twice on the trail here, but she had become too weak and I believe her milk may have dried up. I was getting low on cloth as I kept changing Mercedes bandages; hopefully she would be up to travelling.

As I finished the last of that first cup, I heard a slight noise in the cave. I walked back in and the light from the fire, after catching up the wood I had added to it, shone baby Emma awake. Thinking she might be hungry when she awoke, I had a bottle ready. She smiled at me as I handed her the bottle, very able to hold it herself, so I begin the task of changing her—not really a job I look forward to, but not too much different than changing a saddle and blanket on a horse. It seemed to me it needed to be cinched up tight, just like a saddle; neither needs to come loose at the moment when it is needed most.

2

Mercedes

Looking through a fog in my head, I see the large man knelt over me with Emma lying on my chest, his very large hands are gently lying on us, and he is praying.

Then he is lifting me from a horse, carrying me effortlessly, and gently sitting me against the trunk of a large tree; there he places Emma in my arms, and I feed her.

As I am feeding Emma, there is a dog lying close against me, her head on my legs. I don't mind; she is warm. There is another dog walking behind the large man as he climbs to the top of a ridge just above us.

From the top of the ridge, he looks around, looks down at me and Emma. Then he turns away from us, removes the rifle from his shoulder, and leans it against a tree. He kneels down as the dog sits beside him; he lays one hand on the dog and reaches the other hand toward the sky. I hear something I have not heard any man but a priest do: pray.

"Lord, hear my prayer today, I need your guiding hand, show me the way. These ladies need your protection. It would seem to me you have led me across their path for that reason. I accept the task at hand and, Lord, I feel a certain amount of honor that you would choose me, but in myself I am not enough. The mother needs healing in her body and strength from you, so give it to her. Please, dear Lord, we need a place to hole up for a time of rest and healing. Lead me to this place. And, Lord, there may be men following us. Can you slow them down until I have these ladies at a safe place? Also, Father, forgive me again for the hurt I put on those men."

As I awake, there is the smell of smoke from a fire and the smell of coffee; also, the two dogs are on either side of me. The fog in my head has cleared. I see the large man bent over Emma, her looking up at him and smiling, while his large hands are having a time putting a diaper on her. Seems a little like he was cinching a saddle on a horse.

There were times I remember almost like in a dream, the pain was so unbearable. I feel myself thinking, *Am I dying? Where is Emma?* Then I would hear his voice. He would be praying again, the dogs would nudge close and make small noises, the pain went away, and I would sleep again. Not sure how many times this happened, but each time there was a prayer and a touch.

"Eli, that coffee smells good." When I spoke, both dogs' heads came up and they jumped to their feet and nudged me with their noses. As they were about to lick me, Eli says with voice of command, "Sit," they both sit back on their haunches.

"Ma'am, how do you feel?"

"Good, thanks to you, better, I think."

"Well, ma'am, drink this cup of coffee. It always makes me feel better."

"Eli."

"Yes, ma'am."

"Please call me Mercedes."

"Okay, I will."

The coffee tasted so good; strong for my taste but good. I had sat up and finished the coffee when Emma crawled over to me. Holding her, I could tell she was sleepy and with a little rocking would fall asleep for a midmorning nap.

"Eli, I need you to know why those men were after me and Emma."

"That's your business, Mercedes; you don't have to tell me."

"You should know what you have gotten yourself into, and you deserve to know since you saved my life."

"Mercedes, if I had come along sooner maybe I could have saved the man tied to the wagon wheel. Was he your husband?"

"No, Eli, he was not, but he was a good man. He was helping us to get away. He died bravely, and I am sad for that. He had been a ship's captain and had known my family for many years. I will miss him. My youngest son is named after him."

"Ma'am, you have other children?"

"Yes, three sons. John Paul is twenty-one soon, Emmett is eighteen, and Samuel is fifteen. All tall strong men like their father."

As baby Emma fell asleep in my arms, talking of my sons took me to a place far away with the boys around me. Good men, every one, like their father. The warmth of Emma in my arms and the calm sleeping noises she was making, I began to feel the tiredness in my body.

"You don't have to tell me all this now."

Hearing his voice snapped me back to now, and I knew in my spirit, so I spoke it out: "My sons will find me!" Sleep overtook me then. I felt him pull a blanket over us and I knew the dogs were close, ever watchful, and we were safe.

3

John Paul

I listened close as the man at the bar told of a large man with a long black coat and two vicious dogs tearing into their camp with no fear of who he might hurt, and them just sent to escort the lady and her child to New Orleans.

I moved closer to the bar to hear better. The more the man at the bar and his friend drank, the larger the man became and the more vicious became the dogs.

"Poor Mr. Ewell's eye, he most likely will lose it or be blind in it. All because she refused to let us help her. I never saw a woman so strong and beautiful. She's the big man's problem now, whoever he was, good riddance. Do you know how much trouble we had gittin' Mr. Ewell to come back downriver to New Orleans? Well, I tell ya, if not for him being unconscious most of the way and we knowing we would not be paid till we got back with him, we'd have left him there. He wanted us to go after them, no sir. But I heard him talking to some of the men that had worked for him before. They was told to start gathering some men. When he is better, he will head back upriver after her."

A few questions along the docks and it was easy to find out that Mr. Ewell was the man to hire if you needed someone hurt or just about any unpleasant business takin' care of. Seems even most of the law in New Orleans left him alone from fear, and it was understood he was backed by someone of great influence and money.

Listening more to the men at the bar, I had learned the location of where the story of the woman, the dogs, and the big man had happened. With this information,

I could return to the ship and tell my brothers where we could begin a search for our mother.

I walked from the alley to the dock. There loomed before me the *Mercedes*. A three-mast clipper, I enjoy looking at its lines from the shore. Named by my grandfather, after our mother. She had learned navigation from her father and had sailed many a voyage as navigator with her husband. When we children came along, she decided to stay ashore and leave the sea to our father. She does not know of his death.

When Saul and I went to the house, Mother and baby Emma were gone. But knowing her, there would be a note.

It still seems like a dream to me.

I had just come on deck. There was a rough sea and I could not sleep, looking aft toward the bridge where I knew Father would be. There were two men facing him. One suddenly swung a club, knocking him down. Then before I could run up the stairs to the bridge, I saw them grab him and throw him overboard. I dropped to my knees in disbelief. Suddenly I am aware of men rushing past me and laying hold of the two men.

"John ... Sir, John Paul!" The first mate Saul is talking to me. "Myself and two other mates saw these men attack the captain and throw him overboard. The sea is rough and the dark ... Lad, your father is gone."

Slowly standing, looking around, all the crew was on deck now. Coming face-to-face with these two men, I remembered they were the last men Father had hired on. I wondered why, they did not seem like seamen to me, but he said they needed work. He was always one to give someone a chance if he thought they needed it. He also taught me that the law on a ship had to be fair and just punishment decided by the crew.

"Why did you men attack the captain? My father." Silence; neither had a word to say, just a dead stare. "Men, what say ye?"

Together every man shouted, "Overboard, Captain."

Captain? I looked directly into the eyes of Saul. "John Paul, I knew you since you was born. Captain Ramos always said you would be the captain someday."

Saul was respected by my father, the men on board respected him; some even feared him because of his strength. He is dark and my father said Moorish; North Africa had been his home as a boy.

I saw the fear in the two men's eyes as I nodded my head to the men holding them; then, as they dragged them to the same deck rail they threw Father from, I raised my hand to stop them. "Why did you kill my father?"

Neither man seemed eager to talk. Saul in one quick movement reached to one of the men, grabbed him by his belt buckle and the collar of his shirt in his large hands, lifted him, and threw him into the dark, rough sea. Turning toward the other man, Saul's tall dark figure loomed over him.

"A man named Mr. Ewell gave us money with the promise of more and land deeded to us if we sign on to this ship and killed Captain Ramos."

"Where can I find this Mr. Ewell and how will I know him?" I said.

"He's a big man, nearly as large as your first mate, with bright red hair and beard. He owns a number of saloons in New Orleans. The one he has his office in is the Royal."

"Saul, I will be in the captain's cabin. Come see me when you are done here, please." Turning my back to the man, I stepped down to leave the deck and heard his yell into the dark as Saul and the rest of the men carried out the punishment.

Saul entered the cabin after knocking; he could tell John Paul had been crying. But Saul, with his back straight and eyes ahead, addressed him as he would have his father, Captain Ramos.

"What are your orders, Captain?"

"It does not feel right, Saul, you calling me captain."

"But you are the captain now, and I will serve you as I did your father."

"Okay, Saul. Thanks, but relax. I know my father was also like a father to you. How old were you when he first took you on board?"

"Ten. I was ten years old. My family had been taken by slave traders and I was a beggar in the streets of Casablanca. Captain Ramos gave me my name and taught me my trade. So yes, my father he was, and I will be by your side, John Paul, as long as you let me. Always."

"Saul, my father thought of you as much his son as he did me and my brothers. The men will look to you for leadership. I know we are close to the same age, and I will have to prove myself as their captain. We are three days out from New Orleans. Turn the ship about. When in port, you will accompany me, and we will go to my mother's house and tell her of my father's, her husband's, death. My brothers had left on a trip to Port Arthur, Texas, sailing on another ship owned by Father. They were bringing back a load of cattle. We may have to wait on their return or send someone after them."

4

Emmett

In a moment, a man's life can be changed forever. I read the letter from Mother given to me by the telegraph operator. When we had sailed from New Orleans, she said she would send me a telegram, and I was to send her one back to let her know Samuel and I had arrived safe. This was our first trip away from home without her or our father.

I read the telegram with Samuel looking over my shoulder: Boys, look out for each other. I love you both, maybe Samuel the most. Just like Mother, always kidding about which one of us was her favorite.

I handed the telegram to Samuel, and he smiled as he read it. "I am her favorite, Emmett, see." The telegraph machine began to tick away with a new message for someone as we stepped out of the office to the sidewalk.

"Mr. Ramos," the telegraph operator hollered after us, "there is another message just in for you."

He stepped back up to the operator's desk and handed me the message.

"Another message from Mother?" Samuel said.

"It's from John Paul."

"How can that be, Emmett? He is at sea with Father."

The message read: Father killed at sea. Mother and Baby Emma disappeared. Please return home as soon as possible. Please reply.

"Mister. Can you send this message? will return to ship and make plans to return."

After sending the message, I turned to see Samuel leaving the office. Outside, I found him slumped down against the front of the building, still holding the telegraph. As I stood in front of him he looked up at me, his eyes watered. "Emmett, Father gone, Mother, baby Emma?"

"Samuel, Mother and Father raised us to be strong. Not easy, now, but I just received another message from John Paul. He says he may know where Mother has gone or is headed. We need to find a way to get home as soon as possible. He said he will wait for us. He believes Mother may be okay."

Upon returning to the ship, we showed the telegrams to the captain, a good man who took the news of Father lost with much grief in his face. The ship he sailed belonged to Father, and in his words, "Captain Ramos saved me from a life of drunken chaos, gave me a fresh start by trusting me and having faith in me. So what do you boys need from me? As you can see, the cattle are being loaded onboard now. Should we stop and set sail? Now consider this, boys. Not loaded with cattle, it will take us a week to get back to New Orleans.

But if you boys go book passage on that steamboat *Josephine* you could be in New Orleans in two days."

"Thanks, Captain Glenn. When we get home and sort things out, we'll leave a message for you. We are sure John feels the same as us. You are the captain of this ship as long as you want the position."

"Thanks, boys. Men, you make your father, my friend, Captain Ramos proud. I know this news of your father and mother is tough. Just know that anything you need from me, you have only to ask."

5

Ewell

When a man is strong and smarter than anyone he knows, things come easy to him and he becomes used to having his way. The pain in my right eye will forever remind me of that woman. The doctor told me to always wear a patch to keep the dirt out of it. He said the milky look of it would most likely remain, even though I might regain some sight back in it. Keeping a patch on it was no problem; my vanity would keep me from showing in public the eye that looked awful and felt worse. When I find her, I will repay her for my pain.

I don't remember very much about the trip from Arkansas back to New Orleans. The men who brought me back told the doc I had been a lot of trouble. Good thing I had not paid them or I'm sure they would have left me. Never pay a man till the job is done; don't pay him at all if some excuse can be made. These men did get me back home, but our task with Mercedes Ramos was not accomplished. If they press me I will pay them, but only if they are willing to finish the job.

I may need to have a meeting with the group to discuss our next step concerning the sons. I was told the oldest son had been in my saloon while some of the worthless loudmouthed men I had working for me told about our encounter with his mother. I would silence these men. Then I will find out the plans of this son and where his brothers are.

Stepping from the doctor's office and into the cool morning air felt good, and I could smell the salt from the harbor. Two weeks in bed, the fever broke, the pain in the eye tolerable. Now back to the Royal, to my office, and going over the books of my businesses to see who has been stealing from me. All five of my saloons have managers and they all seem to be making money, but I know if I don't accuse one of them of stealing from me every now and then, they won't think I'm watching.

As I sat at my desk I heard a faint knock at the door once, then twice more. "Come in if you're there. Be quick, I'm busy." The door opened slowly, and he slowly moved into the room, leaving the door open, thinking he might need a quick exit.

The little man I had used before to gather information along the docks; a little money and a bottle of the cheap liquor I sell and he would give information on his own mother, I believe.

Standing, I bent over and opened one of the desk drawers and removed a bottle of liquor, sitting it on my desktop. I walked to the door and closed it. This made him nervous, but that is why I put the bottle on the desk, to help him focus. "The bottle is yours, Claude, go ahead and take it. Have a seat. You can drink it after you tell me what you have learned. Also, there could be some money if I like your information."

Claude reached for the bottle then held it to his chest. "Mr. Ewell, I was very sorry to hear about your eye."

"Never mind about that, Claude. What have you learned about the ship and the Ramos family?"

"Well, Mr. Ewell, Captain Ramos is dead and two other men died onboard. Captain Ramos's oldest son, John Paul, is captain now. Around the docks he is well liked, and it is said he is like his mother, not someone to trifle with. As to what happened to Captain Ramos and those two other men, all the men onboard are being very close-lipped and suspicious of anyone asking questions. I did see some naval officers go onboard the *Mercedes*. I also found out that Mrs. Ramos and her daughter are missing, no one has seen them for weeks."

"Anything else, Claude?"

"Yes, the two younger brothers had gone to Texas to buy cattle, but they are on their way here by way of the *Josephine*."

"Okay, Claude, here's four bits. You may leave now."

I loomed over Claude, between him and the door, my one good eye piercing. That eye and the black patch over the other one, along with my size, would cause any man to fear me. "Claude, if I hear you have spoken to anyone else of our conversation, I will find you. The results of that meeting will not be pleasant for you."

He slipped from the chair, walked around Mr. Ewell, and went through the door allowing it to close behind him. Clutching the bottle tightly, Claude knew his life would always be worthless if he continued to deal with Mr. Ewell. But he knew his life was not worth much anyway; the only time the pain went away was when he had enough liquor in his belly, but it seems like the amount it takes is always more.

My office is on the second floor of the Royal with a window that overlooks the street in front of the saloon. There is a side room with a door to an outdoor stairway leading down to the alley behind the Royal. This room is used for a group of my most trusted men to come and go—a private room with a private exit, very useful to conduct my certain kind of business.

I stepped into the room to find five of those men sitting around the table; I had sent word to them from the doctor's office that I would be in my office and I had a job for them. They all nodded, but no one really showing respect. These men only respected one thing: money being paid for the job. These men were not like the men I had taken upriver with me; they had to be paid up front, but no job or concern of who got hurt mattered, just the pay. We understood each other.

"Okay, men, I have two jobs. These jobs will be worth three hundred dollars up front and two hundred more when the jobs are complete."

"Clem, Joe, here is your money. There are two fresh horses in the stable out back, saddles, and gear with supplies."

"What's the job, boss?" says Clem.

"I need you men to find the whereabouts of a Mrs. Ramos and her child. I'm sending you men because y'all saw the painting of her in the Ramos house when we searched it. Ride up into Arkansas. You should pick up the trail just north of Hopefield, which is the ferry landing across the river from Memphis. Now when you find her, one of you find a telegraph office, and send me a message which says 'we have your package.' Very important no names are mentioned. Start now. I will be waiting for your message." Both men picked up their money, stood from the table, and left the room.

"Udell, Seth, Sam, the job I have for you is to watch the ship in the harbor, the *Mercedes*, and her captain, John Paul Ramos. Find out about his two brothers, their whereabouts. If they leave New Orleans to find their mother, you are to follow them, and cause them as much trouble as you can. Do not let them find her or her child, their sister. Do whatever it takes; hire more men, if you need to. Just report back to me if they leave town. Take your money and go."

With these plans under way, now I just needed to be patient; hopefully, the group of investors I have will see that I am working to accomplish their plans. They made it clear in our last meeting that the money they have invested in my businesses gives them the rights to take over the businesses if need be. But I have noticed that people who have dealings with this group don't just go out of businesses—they disappear. I have never actually met any of them, only their agents. All of these meetings were at night; always five men, one did all of the talking. By his speech, he seemed well educated.

All five were mounted well and armed heavily. In those meetings, one man had a leather satchel of cash. Instructions were given as to how to invest the cash. Lately I had been buying land for them, worthless land, swampland just outside of New Orleans.

I'll take their money and follow their instructions for now. Besides my salary from running these businesses, I have been skimming money and putting it in the safe in my office and in a hidden safe in my house. With this money, I believe I may be able to buy the loyalty of enough men, when my plan to double cross these investors is in place.

The next information I need is why they want the Ramos shipping business and the very large land holdings of Mrs. Mercedes Ramos. Her husband was taken care of. When I made him an offer on his ships, he laughed at me and dismissed me as not serious.

Father from an early age told me if you want something, take it, and then make people believe you deserved it. Over the years, I have practiced this craft;

if you tell a lie as the truth enough times people will believe it. Respectability can be bought.

Mother was always reading me fairy tales from her Bible, but she was weak, body and mind, that's what Father told me many times. One day, she was gone when I came home from school. Father never had much to say about her leavin', just good riddance and we don't need her. She took her Bible with her. I needed her, at least I did then, but over the years I grew to hate her for leavin', and that grew into not caring 'bout or trusting other women.

When the time is right, I might marry when I have enough money, and because of my position I need a wife to serve me, and for appearances, respectability, and such.

I had thought at one time that Mercedes Ramos may have been that woman if I removed her husband from the picture. That had been part of my smaller plan within the group's bigger plan. Whatever it is remains to be seen.

The few times I had tried to talk to her socially, she was kind but clearly not interested. She was well respected in New Orleans for her business sense, helping her husband run their shipping line, and as a mother. Her sons were well known for their manners.

No matter now; she ruined whatever chance she had with me. When my men find her, I will see her one last time.

6

John Paul lifted his hand toward his brothers as they stepped from the *Josephine* to the dock. Saul noticed the expressions on Samuel's and Emmett's faces, very much the same as John Paul's, sad with concern for each other, but anger as well. God help whoever is behind their father's death, and the seeming abduction of their mother and sister.

Saul looked at them and thought to himself, *I watched these boys grow up; they all three inherited their father's strength and both their parents' smarts, but the anger I have seen in them all comes from their mother. Most beautiful woman I ever knew, and like a mother to me, but if that fire in her eye is directed at you, look out. Captain Ramos was the only one who could calm her down quickly with just a few soft words, but that was his way. I miss him.*

"John Paul, how was Father killed, and where are Mother and Emma?" asked Samuel, looking around the dock and laying a hand on both of his brother's shoulders.

John Paul said, "Let's go home and I can tell you everything I have learned. We are being watched here, I am sure. Saul, will you take care of that matter now? We will come to the ship later this evening."

Saul looked toward two men who had been leaning against a large bale of cotton and gave them a nod. As these men stood and turned to walk away, Emmett and Samuel noticed they were part of the crew of the *Mercedes*. Then all of a sudden, they were running toward two men; one had been on the *Josephine* with them and the other seemed to have been waiting for him. Both had been doing a poor job of trying to watch the

Ramos brothers without being obvious. They quickly ducked into an alley with the two from the *Mercedes* right after them. With half a grin and a wink, Saul said, "Got to go, boys. See you back at the ship." Saul walked down the same alley.

"What was that all about?" said Emmett.

"Tell you later," said John Paul, "when we get to the ship."

Walking into the house, Emmett and Samuel could tell, just like John Paul did when he first entered their home, someone had gone through the house looking for something. They had tried to put things back so no one might notice, but this was their home so they noticed everything out of place.

The three brothers were thinking the same thought: *what about Momma's safe place?* In her kitchen were two cooking stoves. One was a large wrought-iron six-burner, with a large oven. The other stove was a very beautiful, white ceramic-front two–burner; the door to the oven of the small stove would not open unless you lifted the right burner plate off and reached down toward the front of the stove and moved a lever.

Once John Paul had the stove door open, they found an envelope lying on top of the paper and money that were normally in her safe. The letter in the envelope written in their mother's handwriting read:

James, my husband; John Paul, Emmett, and Samuel, my sons,

Emma and I, with the help of Captain Samuel, have left. We are headed to the place we spoke of after we sell the ships. There is a man, Lithell Ewell, very dangerous, and the men behind him. Fearing for the life of your sister is why I left. Find us.

You are all my favorite; know that I love you very much.

After each brother read the note from their mother, John Paul was the first to speak. "I know where this

Chapter 6

Mr. Ewell is, and before reading this note from Mother I had plans to take the men from the ship, go find him, and make him answer for having Father killed and for the harm he may have brought on Mother and Emma. Then the patience that Father always tried to teach me slowed me down at least to wait for you two, and now with this note I believe we should go find our mother and sister. Samuel, Emmett, do you agree?"

Both brothers together said yes.

"John Paul," said Emmett, "we know where she was headed. Let's leave now."

"We are taking the *Emma*," said Samuel.

"Boys, gather what you may need from the house, and then we will head down to the ship. It is three o'clock," John Paul said as he looked down at his father's watch.

"How do you have Father's watch?" asked Samuel. "He was never without it."

John Paul handed the open watch to Samuel, who looked at the picture of his mother inside the cover.

Then he handed it to Emmett. After a few minutes of holding the watch and looking at the picture, Emmett handed the watch back to John Paul. With a crack in his voice, Emmett said, "You told us those two men threw Father overboard, so how did you come to have his watch?"

"The evening Father died, before he went up on deck, he gave me his watch and told me to come and relieve him at midnight. The watch was in my vest pocket when I went on deck and saw those two men throw him overboard."

He placed the watch back in the pocket of the leather vest his mother had given him for his twenty-first birthday. The three young men stood in silence.

With a deep breath in and out, John Paul said, "Let's go to the ship now, and yes, we are taking the *Emma*. I have been having the men unload some of the supplies from the *Mercedes* to the *Emma*. 'Course, we were fully stocked on supplies for the voyage we started. I believe it would be best for us to leave after dark.

The fewer who know we are gone and what direction we took, the better."

Stepping onboard the *Mercedes*, Samuel and Emmett were immediately surrounded by every man who wanted to tell them they were sorry about Captain Ramos. This crew had worked for Captain Ramos many years, and the boys had been on a number of voyages with him.

After the men went back to work loading the *Emma*, the three brothers followed Saul's lead down into the lower cargo part of the ship. On entering, there were a few lanterns burning, casting some strange shadows of two men, their hands tied together above their heads and the ropes looped over the main beam. Both men's toes were barely touching the floor. These were the two given chase by the crewmen and Saul, whom Samuel and Emmett had noticed on the dock.

"Captain," said Saul, "these two men have been very cooperative. This little one here is Claude, the other Joe. Now Claude here has been paid to just watch our ship, but for about a month or so he was paid to watch your mother and her comings and goings. Joe here had a slightly bigger job."

The ropes holding up the two men went over the beam and were tied to a support post in the middle of the room. Saul reached up and took hold of the rope holding Joe between the post and the beam. He pulled on the rope, lifting Joe off the floor, causing a grunt from him and a little more fear in the eyes of Claude.

"Joe has actually been paid to follow Samuel and Emmett on their trip and at some point, kill them, making it look like some sort of accident, of course. Both working for Lithell Ewell."

"Now Saul," said John Paul. "I did say not to hurt these men. Just hold them and question them about why they were following us and who was paying them to do it. These men look like they've been in a brawl."

"Well," said Saul, "Captain John Paul, you may not believe this, but these two men did not want to come with us at first, but some harsh discussion and they came and, Captain, you would not believe how clumsy they are. Both slipped and fell on the main deck twice. Apparently, it is hard to walk downstairs with your hands tied behind your back. Claude here fell down the stairs, then Joe, landing on top of Claude. Once we got them strung up down here, it was amazing how they answered every question."

"Okay, Saul no more harm is to come to them." Turning to the two men, John Paul said, "In the morning, my men are going to put you two on the *Josephine* on its way to Texas. If I hear of you two being involved with any more harm to my family …." He paused and lowered his head, the room quiet, and just the creaking of the ship could be heard. "My father would say, if he were here, you men deserve a second chance. Stay away from the drink and find honest work and, above all things, keep it right between you and God. The men on this ship cared deeply for my father Captain Ramos, so by association with the man or men who had him killed, you are lucky to be alive."

Looking down from the stern deck of the ship, John Paul watched as the men were loading supplies on the *Emma*. It was a stern-wheeler, steam-powered paddleboat sixty feet long and twenty-four feet wide with a very shallow draft, only drawing about three feet of water when loaded. The builder of the boat told Father when he bought it that he believed it could navigate on heavy dew.

Emmett stood beside John Paul. Both were looking down at the *Emma* and watching Samuel direct the men, having them shift the load around the boat to more evenly distribute the weight.

"John Paul, I believe Father would be glad we are using the *Emma* to go after and find Mother and baby sister, since he bought it for me and Samuel to start our own business carrying supplies and goods up small rivers off the Mississippi."

"Captain John Paul," said Saul as he walked up toward the brothers, "your boat is loaded and ready for your trip. There is a large supply of wood for the engine. As I understand from river men I have talked to lately, there are men along the river who cut wood and sell it to steamboats upriver, so y'all should have no problem with fuel. Will there be anything else, Captain?"

"Yes, Saul, there is. Here are papers making you captain of the *Mercedes*. Samuel, Emmett, and I, as you know, are going to find our mother. I ... we would like you to sail the ship with the tide and finish the voyage Father started. In Father's will I was given all rights to this ship, so I have signed these papers naming you captain if you will accept."

Saul's tall dark figure stood very straight; his eyes grew even darker than normal. With John Paul standing six foot one, Saul was a good head taller. He had said once, of the men from his tribe, he was not tall. Saul extended his hand to John Paul, still not speaking, just looking at him with those dark eyes.

"Your father was my father, and you three men are my brothers. I pledge my life to you and your family. It would be my honor to be the captain of the *Mercedes*."

"Depending on the trade route you take, I believe you will be back to New Orleans in six- to-eight months. When you do return, unload all the cargo in our warehouse. If we are not here to meet you there will be a message at the telegraph office. If everything goes all right, the original plan by Father was that the goods brought back on this voyage would be sold upriver on the *Emma*."

Suddenly the night around seemed bright. John Paul turned to see the *Emma* was on fire.

There was a large group of men holding torches on the dock next to the *Emma*. John Paul and Emmett watched as Samuel jumped from the *Emma* to the dock with a long push pole from the boat. He struck one of the men holding a torch between the eyes, and began swinging the pole in all directions in the middle of the crowd of ruffians. In just moments, the crew from the

Mercedes was on the dock and it seemed like the entire New Orleans waterfront was in one large brawl.

Running to help their brother, and after laying a few ruffians out themselves, they—John Paul, Emmett, and Samuel—ran toward the *Emma*. Untying her moors, they jumped onboard and began to put out the fire. Most of the fire started by the thrown torches came from a large oilskin tarp on deck covering a supply of wood. Cutting the tarp loose and throwing it overboard, most of the fire went with it, leaving just a few pieces of wood smoldering.

Samuel had the steam up when the fire had started, so while the others were making sure the fire was out, he engaged the paddle wheel, and the *Emma* began to leave the dock, with the sound of the paddle wheel churning water and pushing the boat into the dark.

Two men noticed the *Emma* leaving the dock. Saul stepped to the edge of the dock, taking hold of each man by the collar. "Go with God, my brothers." Then he threw both men in the water. The other man stood back in the shadows, watching as the men of his saloons were being scattered and beaten down by the crew of the *Mercedes*.

Even back in the shadows as he watched the boat slip into the darkness, the hate could be seen in his eye.

7

Awaking suddenly and finding Emma not beside her, a fear gripped her. Seeing light at the entrance to the cave, she ran. Standing there under the large rock overhang, looking down toward the river, she saw a sight that immediately relieved her of fear. Standing in the middle of a small patch of grass was Emma, both of the dogs—Bill and Mary-Lou, she believed Eli had called them—were jumping all excited around her, reaching out to one then the other, gently touching her with their noses. This made her squeal with delight. Every time she would begin to fall, the dogs would move in close and she would grab hold of them and steady herself. When they felt like she was steady, they would back away and the game would start all over. All going on under the watchful eyes of Elijah. She could hear him saying through a large grin, "Y'all be careful with her, she is just a baby." As he said this, he turned and noticed Mercedes standing at the entrance to the cave. In a tone you would use for a good friend, he called the dogs by name, and they both stopped their game with Emma and looked up at him. "Good dogs." Then he stretched his large hands toward Emma. She looked at him and smiled even bigger than she was, then reached her small hands toward him. Elijah lifted her effortlessly to his shoulders, where she grabs two handfuls of his thick hair to hold on to as they walked up the hill to her mother.

The dogs ran up the hill ahead of them. When they got to Mercedes, they sat on either side of her; she knelt down between them and greeted them both with a gentle rub on their backs. When she stood up, Elijah and Emma had made it up the hill. Emma immediately released her hold on his hair and dived from his shoulders to the arms of her mother.

"How are you feeling, ma'am?"

"Very well, Elijah, thanks to your doctorin', and please call me Mercedes. I have not been much of a mother to Emma these past few days, but you and she seem to have formed quite a relationship. She looks well cared for, thank you. Not many men I know would have been capable of such a task."

"Well, Mercedes, I have done my best for y'all. With some help from a higher power, we have made it this far. I believe you will find Ms. Emma there is ready for a nap, being how it is ten o'clock this morning and she has been up since dawn."

Emma's eyes were heavy looking, so Mercedes turned to walk back into the cave to lay her down on a blanket beside the small fire. This had been her regular nap time back home when things were normal. Looking around the cave, she was amazed how in the few days they had been in the cave Elijah had made it seem safe. Emma took to the blankets, and within just a few minutes, she was asleep. The dogs had wanted to follow her into the cave but Elijah had not let them; he thought they might disturb her sleep.

Coming out from the cave, Mercedes brought with her the coffeepot and two cups. She filled both cups and sat the pot behind the big rock Elijah was sitting on. She sat on a rock facing him and pulled the leather pouch from under her arm, the one he had brought from the wagon.

"Eli, I want to tell you why that man was after me and Emma."

"You don't have to; it is your business."

"No, you deserve to know what trouble you have brought on yourself by helping us. In this leather pouch are a birth certificate and a will that a man named Lithell Ewell would do anything to get his hands on. Can you tell me, is he still alive?"

"I believe he could be, Mercedes, but I am certain wherever he is, he is in pain, because of you."

"Good. I wish harm on no one, but I had to protect Emma. Mr. Ewell had tried, on a number of occasions, to buy into our business. John, my husband, had turned him down politely at first, telling him his sons would take over the business someday."

"What sort of business are you and your husband in?"

"We own two three-mast clipper ships with a warehouse in New Orleans. The two ships make regular trips to England, France, and Africa. Taking cotton and wheat with them and bringing back many different commodities, which I sell to merchants in New Orleans mostly. But recently, my husband has wanted to expand, so he bought a small steam-powered paddleboat to start bringing supplies up the White River. We even bought a piece of land on the river in the Ozarks, close to a small town call Oakland. My husband's thinking was maybe we would build a dock for steamboats, and maybe we would become part of the small town, move inland and leave the sea. He talked about it from when

I first told him I was going to have a baby. Our two younger sons did not seem to have the love of the sea that their older brother did, so my husband felt that he would leave the *Mercedes*—the ship he is the captain of—to John Paul, and we would move to Oakland. Just a dream at that point.

"Back to Mr. Ewell. When John left for his last voyage, Emma and I stood on the dock and watched the ship disappear over the horizon. John Paul, my oldest, was on the ship with his father, and the day before, the two younger boys had sailed on our other ship to Texas to buy beef. *He* was waiting for us at the house.

"There he sits in my living room, two very rough-looking men standing on either side of him. With a smile and an air that I was doing him a favor just to be in his presence, he says, 'Mrs. Ramos, I have made a few very generous offers to you and your husband. Now I have information that your husband may not return from this voyage and your sons may not return from Texas. So here is my latest offer. You and your daughter may come and live with me. You will be well cared for and your business will become part of mine. Now, I'll give you some time to consider, so no reason to give me a decision right away, but I have some papers here on your table. These documents sign the ownership of the business to me, and this one document makes me the legal guardian of your daughter. I will be back tomorrow for your decision.'

"I knew by him wanting to be Emma's guardian he had found out about the will. My father had owned hundreds of acres of land around New Orleans. When he died, in his will he left all of his land to me, except for a few hundred acres of seemingly worthless swamp. In his will, it states, 'This hundred acres of swampland left to my youngest grandchild so far unborn, the sale or management of this land by her parent or legal guardian.' This land joins the New Orleans docks. The New Orleans port is expanding rapidly after the Civil War, so this swampland is worth millions if sold and much more if leases are to be used to expand the port.

The city council has already approach us, and we were working with a lawyer in New Orleans to see how to proceed. All of the money would be put in a trust for Emma. I believe Mr. Ewell found out about the will from the lawyer firm we have been using.

"When he and his men left, I knew I had to leave, too. So after I was sure they were out of sight, I took Emma and I went to Samuel's house."

"The man tied to the wagon wheel," said Elijah.

"Yes. Are you sure he was gone, Eli?"

"I'm sorry, he was. I checked him to make sure. There was nothing to be done for him. I know he had been a special friend to you, and you told me earlier he had worked for your father."

With a look of sadness on her face she continued. "When I told Samuel of my encounter with Lithell Ewell, he agreed we should leave town. He told me to go pack and he would go acquire us passage on the next steamboat going up the Mississippi.

"When we arrived in Memphis, Samuel purchased us a wagon and team and supplies. We boarded a ferry to the Arkansas side of the Mississippi, thinking we might escape, but Lithell had people watching me when I left. So he followed and had caught up to us a few hours before you found us, Eli."

"So, Elijah, there is the trouble you are a part of. If you wish to leave us at the next town or point me in the direction to the closest town, I would understand. I am now, thanks to your doctorin', well enough to travel. When I am at a town that has a telegraph office, I will send some messages to locations I believe my husband and sons may be when they start looking for me, if they are alive."

"Here is the thing, Mrs. Ramos, I know your husband."

A look of question fell on Mercedes's face. "How, Eli?"

"I met Captain John Ramos, your husband, in England, when I was looking for an American ship headed for New Orleans. On the voyage over, we spent many an evening talking. I ate my supper in the captain's cabin most nights, and so did your oldest son, John Paul, a soon-to-be-captain of his own ship, I think. A well-spoken young man, a credit to his raisin', I believe, a sure reflection of his parents."

"Thank you, Eli. He is a wonderful young man, a little more like his father than me. May I ask what your business was in New Orleans, Eli? And why you were in England? I'm sorry, Elijah, it's okay if you don't want to tell me. You don't seem like the kind of man who likes to talk about himself."

"No, ma'am, and you are right, I don't talk about myself much, but you do have a right to know who you and your daughter are traveling with and what my intentions are.

"After fighting in the war for the first year and then spending two months in a hospital recovering from wounds, I was promoted to the rank of colonel. Soon after the promotion, I was asked to come to

Washington and report to the secretary of state, William H. Seward, for a special assignment. If this story gets too long, Mercedes, or you get tired, just stop me."

"You have my interest, Eli. Secretary of state. Please go on."

"When I was led into the secretary's office, there were two other men there. The first to extend his hand to me was President Abraham Lincoln, but I did not extend my hand to him. I stood straight and saluted him. He would have none of that. He said, 'At ease, soldier, colonel,' with his hand still presented. I shook his hand and he shook back, placing his other hand on my shoulder and leading me into the room. Then he introduced me to Mr. Seward, and also to a Mr. Charles Francis Adams, who I later learned was the son and grandson of two presidents. But at this time, he was the minister to England.

"After we were all seated, some coffee was brought in, which I was very thankful for, since the meeting was set for 7:30 a.m. and I had to leave my quarters early with no time for coffee.

"The secretary begins to tell me about the assignment. I was to accompany Mr. Adams to England and serve as an adviser on military matters. The president explained that the United States needed to keep good relations with England, as we would need them for trade after the war. Also, he felt that a military man with the minister, and my background of studying the law, would be helpful in agreements that we might reach with England. Still not bored? Should I go on?"

"Yes, please do."

"After the war, Mr. Adams decided to return to his political career in the States, and I had decided on a new job. I was on my way to my new position when I came across your troubled camp. From England, I decided to take a ship to New Orleans then a steamboat up the Mississippi then cross country on horseback to a little town on the White River in Arkansas called Oakland."

"Quite a story, Elijah Johnson. So, we are headed to the same town?"

"Yes, ma'am, it seems we are."

"Have you ever been there, Eli?"

"No, I have not, have you?"

"No, but my husband traveled by steamboat to Oakland two years ago. May I ask what your business will be there?"

"I will be the pastor of a new church. They have been having church in a barn and livery stable. I will help them build a building, is the plan."

"Eli, aside from the praying I have seen of you on the trail and when you first found us, I would have thought sheriff would be a job you were more suited for, knowing that somehow you managed to handle those twelve men."

"Well, Bill and Mary-Lou helped some."

"Okay, I'll give the dogs some credit, but how does a fighting man like you—and believe me, I know a little about fighting men, raised on the docks and around sailing men all my life, plus three sons—how does that man become a pastor? Preaching peace and love thy neighbor."

"Are you sure you want more of my story? You're not tired?"

"No, I'm good, Eli, please go on."

As he continued Mercedes took notice of the place he had chosen for them to rest. The sounds of birds, and squirrels barking made the woods around them seem alive. The site was clearly chosen from a military point with clear sight to anyone approaching.

"Okay, because this is the part of my life that I always will discuss with anyone. This is my life when I came to know Jesus Christ as my savior.

"Charles Adams and I were in England for two months, and I found that part of my job as the assistant to the minister of England was bodyguard. An attempt on his life was made on the voyage over and one more attempt a month after we arrived in London. These attempts met with my unforgiving talent to handle anyone who wishes to bring harm to myself or someone close to me. One Sunday, with nothing better to do, I decided to attend a church and listen to a preacher I had been hearing the Londoners speak of. The church was the Metropolitan Tabernacle; the preacher was a young man in his late twenties. His name was Charles Spurgeon.

"After the congregation sang a few hymns, he began his sermon. He spoke with such conviction, and it seemed he was talking to me, as if he knew me, even though the crowd that day was easily over a thousand. Preacher Spurgeon said God knew me and that to live in a right relationship with God I only needed to ask him in the name of Jesus Christ, the son he sent to this earth to die for my sins, to forgive me. Then he went on to explain that no amount of goodness on my own would ever put me in that right relationship with God, so, just ask.

"At the end of his sermon, he invited anyone who would like to know more about a personal relationship with God be in his vestry Monday morning.

"Monday morning I was there. After he invited me in, he asked how he might help me, and I said that right relationship with God he spoke of Sunday, I wanted it. So he opened his Bible to Ephesians chapter two, verse eight: 'For by grace are ye saved through faith: and that not of yourselves: it is the gift of God.' Then he asked me to pray with him and to ask God to forgive me of my sins. I tried to explain to him there were many, being a soldier. He kept saying God will give me this free gift of salvation regardless of my past if I but ask. So we prayed. I asked God to forgive me, went away from his office knowing in my heart I was not the man I had been, now forgiven and in right relationship with my God.

"The rest of my time in London I regularly attended the Metropolitan Tabernacle and was mentored by my friend Charles Spurgeon. Then there came a time one day in prayer when I knew the call to be a pastor was now where God wanted to use me. Through letters with family I have in the area, I found that the small town of Oakland needed a pastor, so I prayed and it just felt right."

From the cave, Emma awoke with a small cry calling for her mother. Mercedes stood to go, and checked her step. She went over to him, laid her hand on his shoulder, and said, "Thanks, Elijah Johnson. I am glad I know your story." Then she turned to see to Emma.

8

Eli

Arriving in Newport, Arkansas, late morning, Mercedes first wanted to locate the telegraph office and send telegrams to her sons and leave a message for them there if they should make it to Newport. Then we went down to the river. There was a steamboat there about to leave and head upriver. Mercedes told me we needed a little good luck, and I told her I had prayed for God's hand on the rest of our journey, so I was looking at the fact that the boat was there waiting on us as an answer to prayer. She agreed.

The boat's name was the *Trader* and it had some cabins available, so I acquired passage for two with two cabins. I was told the trip was an overnight trip; we would arrive in Oakland the next day about this time. We stepped on the boat just as it was ready to leave; it was little after three in the afternoon, and we were told the captain was ready to leave and travel till dark, and then he would moor the boat. Traveling at night on the river is dangerous because of snags and low water.

I was awakened to the feel of the boat moving and the sound of the steam whistle. Lying there, I could hear Emma talking to her mother. Then I heard Mercedes voice telling her, "'lijah and the dogs are just next door" and "come back to bed." Emma didn't have much of a vocabulary yet, so she had started calling me 'Lijah. The walls were thin between the cabins. Bill and Mary-Lou slept just outside both doors to the cabins; of course, they both would have rather been in the cabins, but I knew outside the doors no one would get past them without paying a price. I had dogs growing up, but I never had dogs more protective of me than these two; in the last two weeks of us caring for Emma and Mercedes, they were just as protective of them.

Getting up and washing my face, I decided there would be coffee somewhere on this boat. Stepping from the cabin, I was greeted by the dogs. They quickly took the beef jerky I gave them and then stepped over to a rain barrel, stood on their back legs, and reached in for a drink. As I started to walk away, I turned to see both dogs had gone back to sit in front of the ladies' door. God help anyone who might try and go into that cabin uninvited.

Walking onto the front deck of the boat, I found a small woodstove with a large coffeepot and metal cups; the coffee was strong, just right. Stepping to the railing, the sun had just risen. There was still some fog on the river, but there was a slight southern breeze clearing it away. We were moving at a much slower speed because of the fog; once it was all gone, I was sure the captain would have the paddle really churning water.

After finishing my first cup, I turned to go back to the coffeepot and there stood Mercedes pouring herself a cup. I held out my cup and she poured me another. We both stepped over to the rail to watch the shore go by.

"Emma fell back to sleep soundly with Bill and Mary-Lou at the door. I needed coffee." Our cabin doors faced the front deck we were on. The dogs owned that cabin door. As I watched them, a crew member walked a little too close and stopped in front of them. Both dogs bared their teeth and a low growl was heard; he moved on.

Mercedes said, "I awoke suddenly, early, thinking of John. I'm not one to have fear of what might be, that's from being a ship captain's wife and daughter of a seafaring man, but there is a feeling in me I cannot explain. I know he and John Paul were only a few days gone on their voyage, and Samuel and Emmett a few days gone when we left. I guess I just woke and realized it could be a long time before they even know we are gone."

"I will continue to pray for God's protection on your husband and sons and that they will soon learn where y'all have gone. I will find a safe place for you and Emma to stay in Oakland. Also, we will send messages downriver with every boat that comes by."

We stood in silence for some time just listening to the paddle wheel churning water and watching the shore go by; it seemed to have a calming effect on Mercedes. I could imagine the pain of missing her husband and sons, the not knowing. I still missed my wife and child; the pain never goes away. When one day you realize you will never see them again there is no fix for that pain; only God can, over time, offer some comfort. I hoped she never has to feel that loss. With God's help, I will do my best to somehow help this woman and baby girl to get back with their family.

"Eli, what type of tree with the white flowers is all along the woods there? And some places along the shore, I can see them growing far back into the woods."

"Those are dogwoods, Mercedes, one of my favorite trees. They also grow in Louisiana, northern maybe."

"You may be right. I just never noticed so many in one place growing wild. Why is the dogwood your favorite tree?"

"Interesting you should ask, because tomorrow is Sunday, and I will be able to preach my first sermon in Oakland on Easter Sunday."

"So how does a tree and Easter Sunday relate?"

"There is a legend told in these hills that the dogwood tree was the type of wood the cross they hung Jesus on was made of. So since then its blossoms are in the form of the cross, two long and two short petals. In the center of the outer edge of each petal will be the print of the nails. In the center of the flower, stained with blood, will be a crown of thorns, so that all who see it will remember."

Mercedes noticed that as he told her about the dog-woods, Elijah's voice began to crack some with emotion; seemed hard to believe that a man of such strength and with the ability he had to best those twelve men would now show such emotion and gentleness.

Suddenly the dogs were barking. I turned toward the cabins and there stood Emma, having gotten out of bed and opened the door. Mercedes rushed to her. A small child on deck could easily go overboard.

Later in the early evening, the steam whistle blew and the landing for Oakland was in sight. It had been an easy trip upriver with one stop to take on wood, which gave the dogs a chance to run on shore.

The Oakland landing was really just a bank that the captain nosed the boat into. A wide plank was put down to go ashore. There were twenty or so people there to meet the boat, some just curious and a couple of store owners who had supplies ordered; it seemed to be the main business of the steamboats going upstream and bringing crops downstream on the return trip.

Mercedes carried Emma to shore while I brought the horse from the back of the boat where there was a pen built for livestock. Most people would agree the livestock should be at the back of any boat, thanks to the smell and such that goes along with livestock.

I had been told in a letter there were living quarters for me and a place to hold services. I was to contact a Mr. Kilpatrick, a local store owner. I led the horse down the plank, which, by the way, he did not like the movement of. So I thought for a moment, either I would have to carry the horse to shore or we were going to both end up in the river. The dogs were not helping by standing on shore and barking, but we made it.

Once on shore, I noticed Mercedes was talking to a woman who was sitting up in a buckboard wagon. The crew was loading cargo from the boat to the wagon, and the captain was talking to a man beside it; they seemed to be friends. As I walked up to them, the captain turned to me and said, "Elijah, let me introduce you to my friend and his wife. James and Sarah

Kilpatrick, meet Mr. Elijah Johnson." I extended my hand, and James Kilpatrick took it. A handshake tells a lot of a man, and I could tell even though he had a few years on him, this man was a hard worker. While shaking his hand, I tipped my hat to his wife.

From the seat of the buckboard Mrs. Kilpatrick said, "I have already been talking to Mercedes and her beautiful baby girl. She has explained a little of ya'lls' situation, so I'll give them a ride in the buckboard and you men can follow. Then we'll have a nice talk and get you folks settled."

"Elijah," said the captain, "I sure did enjoy visiting with you last night over a cup of coffee. When I am back in a week, hope you will come down to meet the boat and tell me how you have settled in. I will keep my eye out for the men you spoke of when I get back downstream. Good luck. Looks like we are unloaded."

Once the captain was onboard and the gangplank was drawn in, the stern paddle wheel began to turn in reverse, pulling the boat into the river channel. Then it stopped and began to churn forward, taking the boat upstream.

As the boat moved upriver, James Kilpatrick took notice of this large man standing beside him, a Henry rifle slung across his back and clearly a few more weapons under his long, black-caped coat. He looked more like a lawman than a pastor.

"Mr. Johnson, we have been expecting you for a while, but I will say you are not what I expected."

"Mr. Kilpatrick, the war changed a lot of men. But mostly I was changed by God for the better, I believe. Mr. Kilpatrick?"

"Yes, Mr. Johnson."

"Call me Eli, please."

"Okay, Eli. I will, if you call me James. Come on, let's catch up to the ladies, and I'll show you where you can stable the horse."

Turns out the living quarters were in a barn, which was also where they had been holding church services.

Sarah Kilpatrick took to Mercedes and Emma right off. They had a large house behind their general store with plenty of room, so it was decided the ladies would stay with the Kilpatricks.

The town had a general store, a blacksmith shop, a livery, a restaurant named The Split Pea, and a government land office. Across the road from the land office was a sheriff office. Sheriff Warren had left town with a group of soldiers to look for two men wanted in connection with a number of robberies up and down the river; it was said he should be back in town by Monday. There was a nice couple with five kids, Jeb and Ira Stockton, who had a house and store business on Main Street. Jeb did all kinds of leatherwork, including boot and shoe repair, and his wife, Ira, made dresses and mended clothes. A few houses and that was the town. The barn set on a hill just south of the town overlooking the river. James said there were a lot of families living outside of town and when they hear we have a pastor they will come in for church on Sunday.

After leaving Mercedes and Emma in the care of
Sarah, James first took me and the dogs for the tour of
the barn. One thing he was proud of, and that was a
large church bell he had shipped from St. Louis, Mis-
souri. Until a proper church building was built, the bell
was hanging from a large limb of an oak tree in front
of the barn. People had been told by James to listen for
it; on a Sunday morning, the ringing of it would be an-
nouncing the new pastor. Through the two large doors
were beautiful large hand-hewed beams across and one
main beam down the center; this was not just a barn
but a building built by someone who was good at their
craft. Outside and just to the left of the main doors
was a smaller door leading into a room that could be
used as an office; there were a few chairs and wooden
bench along one wall, then straight through to a nice
bedroom complete with feather bed, wash basin, and
curtains on the two windows. James said the ladies in
town had a hand in fixing the living quarters up, making it seem a little homier. On through the bedroom

there was a door that led into a horse stall that had a half door opening up to the back of the barn and another door opening into the main room. Looked like a good room for the dogs to sleep.

"What sort of services have y'all been having, James?"

"Well, most Sundays we gather and have prayer, someone will read a few chapters from the Bible, and then we will pray again and go home. When we decided we really needed a pastor is when Pastor Luke came over from Hardwood, a nice little town not far from here. He held some revival services for us. Listening to him preach let us know we needed a proper pastor before this town would really have a church. So I talked to him the last time he came over and asked him if he knew any preacher who might be interested. He gave me your name, said you were in England in the military, but in a letter he had last received from you, after leaving the army you were studying to become a pastor and would be looking for a church. I believe he told me you have some kinfolk in Hardwood."

"Pastor Luke and I have remained friends since college where we both studied law before the war and have stayed in touch through letters. He is a good man. The kinfolk I have in Hardwood is name of William O'Brian; he is the grandson of my cousin Colonial O'Brian."

"Yes, I know William and his partner, Thomas," said James. "I have bought timber from them. "There is a striking family resemblance between you and William. My business dealing with him showed me a man raised to be honest and a man whose word given was true."

"The last time I saw him," said Eli, "he was just a boy. I do look forward to getting to know him again and his family. I did write him a letter telling him I would be coming to Oakland to live."

9

John Paul

Easter Sunday and we had the *Emma* tied to the dock at Newport, Arkansas. We should not have been traveling the river as much at night as we had, but the chance had to be taken; we needed to find our mother and sister. Neither of us had slept much this past week, traveling day and night. Luck would have it when we arrived at Memphis and took on wood, we found a man who had traveled the White River looking for a job. Clyde was about sixty years old, I believe, and the years could be read on his face. He seemed much older, but he did know the White River and just how to stay in the channel and avoid the shallow waters. We would check the telegraph office and see if there were any messages, then take part of the day to rest and take on supplies.

"John Paul, the telegraph office is closed. No one around anywhere on Main Street," said Samuel.

Emmett spoke up, saying, "I hear church music. I say the town is all at church."

"We need supplies and we are all tired. How about we take a day off, rest, get our supplies in the morning. Maybe after everyone is out of church we could ask around and see if anyone knows or may have seen Mother pass this way."

"Sounds like a good idea, John Paul," said Samuel. "I could use some shut-eye."

Soon after noon, church let out and the whole congregation came walking down Main Street toward the river, most of them carrying basket and blankets. They turned just north of where we had the *Emma* tied. Along a grassy bank, the lady folk began to spread their blankets and lay out food. Soon a couple of young ladies and a gentleman, who by the badge on his vest would seem to be the sheriff, approached the boat. Both ladies dressed in their bonnets and Sunday best was a welcome sight. They were all smiles, but it was the sheriff who did the talking.

"Men, I am Sheriff Hunt, and these are my two daughters, Anna and Isabelle." At their introduction both girls began to giggle, which brought big smiles on Samuel's and Emmett's faces and a frown on the sheriff's. "Settle down, girls. I need to talk to these men. Who is in charge?"

Everyone onboard looked at me. "Sheriff, my name is John Paul Ramos. These are my brothers, Samuel and Emmett, and this is a river boatman who works for us. He is Clyde Smith."

"I saw you boys come in early this morning. Fact, it was still dark. Mighty dangerous traveling this river at night. I figured y'all would be needing supplies, but the town is closed for Easter Sunday."

"Sheriff, we are looking for our mother and baby sister, which is why we are traveling at night. We believe she may have traveled through here on her way upriver to a place called Oakland."

"Friday, a lady, tall with dark hair and a baby girl, took passage on the *Trader* headed upstream. I know it makes a regular stop at Oakland."

"Did they seem okay, Sheriff Hunt?"

"Yes, I believe so. They were traveling with a big man and two dogs."

"I don't know who that may be, Sheriff."

"They were not in town long; the boat was ready to leave as soon as they were onboard. I did see the big man holding the baby for a while as the lady went up to the telegraph office. The girl seemed very comfortable with the big man. Now, boys, the main reason I came over to your boat was my wife sent me to invite y'all to Sunday lunch. There is more than enough food, and I will be in trouble with my wife and these two girls if y'all don't come eat with us." Samuel and Emmett both jumped from the boat, each offering an arm to the two girls before walking toward the blanket where the girl's mother was waiting with food.

"Sheriff," I said, "my brothers have answered for me and Clyde, so thank you, we accept your offer. The brothers may be tired of my cooking and beef jerky."

"Me too," said Clyde. "I do believe I smell fried chicken."

As we all walked up to the gathering, the pastor was just saying a prayer over the food. After the meal, the pastor of the church waded out into the river and a number of the townsfolk were baptized.

"John Paul, weren't we all sprinkled with holy water by our priest?" said Samuel. "Why does the preacher feel the need to hold those folks all the way under the water?" The one sheriff's daughter, Anna, who had been sitting the closest to Samuel and, I noticed, paying close attention to everything he had to say during the meal, was quick with an answer.

"We are Baptist folk, Samuel, and we believe in total submersion. The old man goes under and a new man comes up. Of course, we also believe a person has already made his amends with Jesus and the baptizing is showing everyone he's a new man."

"Well, our mother seems to believe a good sprinkling with holy water when we were babies was all we needed," said Samuel.

"I hear tell holding some folks underwater for a while might do them some good," said Anna.

Suddenly there seemed to be some tension between Samuel and Anna. There was that quick temper of our mother showing up in Samuel, but in a matter of minutes after Emmett told Samuel he was goin' to drag him out in the river and give him his own long baptizing, he jumped up ready, and both girls began laughing and the mood was okay. Then both brothers invited the girls, if it was all right with their parents, to show them the *Emma*. They walked toward the boat, and suddenly I was glad for this day and the folks we were meeting in this town. For a moment it lifted the dark cloud that was on us, with our father killed and our mother and sister missing. The sheriff and his wife were good folks, and before I knew it I was telling them about our father dying and our mother and sister gone.

"Sheriff, I know it is Sunday, but do you suppose I might talk to the telegraph operator? Maybe if that was my mother, she left a message with him for us."

"Sure, John Paul, I seen him at church, so him and his family should be here somewhere. I am sorry to hear about you boys' dad. That must be hard, and I will keep my eye out for any of the hard case men coming up the river after you leave."

"Thanks, Sheriff."

We found the telegraph operator, and he said if my last name was Ramos there was a message in the office from a Mercedes Ramos, and he would be glad to take me to the office and give it to me.

Dear John, my love, and sons,

If you are reading this message you have come up the river after Emma and myself. I knew you would. There is a heaven-sent man helping us. We are leaving Newport now, Friday evening, March 30th, on a boat; the Trader is its name, headed upriver to a small town called Oakland. We will wait for you there. The man helping us, he was a passenger on your trip back from England; his name is Elijah Johnson. See you soon, I hope."

How will I tell her Father is dead?

10

Eli

Sunday morning Eli awoke in his small room in the back of the barn, the barn that would be his first church to pastor. The small woodstove still had a few embers, just enough to stir up and get a fire going for some coffee. The second cup was tastin' as good as the first cup when both dogs' ears went up and the church bell began a-ringing. As he walked outside, both dogs run past him through the large front double doors of the barn, and he found James Kilpatrick a-pulling the rope and a-ringin' the bell. The dogs jumped around him very excited, barking, or maybe that should better be described as howling, as he rings a few more minutes.

"I know it's early, Pastor Eli, but I just wanted folks back in the hills to have plenty of time to get ready and come to church this morning and hear their new pastor. Now Sarah sent me to fetch you for breakfast. We have time 'cause we don't generally try to start service till about ten. I hope you have a good sermon for this morning, Pastor."

"I hope so too, James. Been up good part of the night studying and prayin' asking God what my first sermon should have for you folks."

After breakfast, I walked back down to the barn church and folks were beginning to gather outside. The dogs ran past me; they loved attention and they saw the children down there in the small crowd that had gathered.

Mercedes and Emma rode in the wagon down to the church with the Kilpatricks. As they pulled up, Mercedes noticed the ease of Elijah in the middle of the group of people he had never met, talking and picking up the children, introducing himself, as well as introducing the dogs by name to the children. As she watched him and listened to him visiting with these families, it was so evident that this man had found his calling and these people needed him. Soon James rang the bell again and everyone began to go into the barn for the service. The pews were rough-cut planks laid across blocks of wood. There was no pulpit, but Elijah seemed very comfortable standing in front of everyone holding his mother's Bible as if he had been doing it for years.

"Folks, I stand in front of y'all today humbled to be called your pastor. Most of you I met out front. My given Christian name is Elijah James Johnson. My friends call me Eli, so please call me Eli.

"I would like to read from God's word and then just talk to you for a while about this life we live. Please stand as I read from the word: first book of Peter, verse three: 'Blessed be the God and Father of our Lord Jesus Christ, which according to his abundant mercy hath begotten us again unto a lively hope by the resurrection of Jesus Christ from the dead.'

"Today is Easter Sunday, folks, the day we celebrate the resurrection of our Lord and Savior Jesus Christ, the living Son of God. Now if everyone will please bow your heads I would like to pray. Lord Jesus, I ask you to open our hearts today to hear and know your will for our lives. Let me, God, only speak by your help and anointing of the Holy Spirit, amen."

"Everyone, please be seated. Life goes on and God cares about everything in your life, from the big events of marriage or a child being born to the sadness of the loss of a loved one, he knows and cares more, I believe, than we can even understand. The Bible tells us he knows when a sparrow falls to the ground and that he has the hairs on our head numbered. Those scriptures about the sparrow falling go on to say how much more he cares about us in this life we live.

"Folks, as y'all get to know me, you will find I'm not much to quote verse and chapter, but if I have made mention of a verse in the Bible and you want to know the location in the scriptures, come see me anytime and we will have us a Bible study. In fact, I believe we need to start a Sunday school for the kids and a class for the adults as well.

"My favorite verses in the Bible are the parts written in red, because these are the words of my Lord and Savior. When Jesus walked this earth, he taught his followers how to live a life free of guilt and shame.

"One story in the New Testament tells of Jesus meeting a woman at a well that she had come to draw water from. He knew she had five husbands and was with a man not her husband, but he did not condemn her. Another woman was brought to him, caught in sin, her accusers ready to stone her. This time Jesus said to her accusers, 'Any among you without sin, cast the first stone.' Then he told the woman, when her accusers had gone, 'Go and sin no more.' He gave these women hope.

"Men and women, I did my time as a soldier in the War Between the States. There is guilt, things I do not speak of, families were lost. God knows and he forgives if we but ask, and he goes beyond the forgiveness, he forgets, the Bible tells me so. My Bible tells me also to forget those things which are behind, and reach forth to those things which are before me. Not easy, my friends, but with God's help there is a bright and hopeful future.

"There are people I will never see again this side of heaven. The sadness of it almost brings me to my knees—and it has, in the past. God gave me this life to live and to reach forth to those good things he has put in front of me. There is someone who needs you; God puts them in your path.

"Here is an example. Perhaps some of you have met Mrs. Mercedes Ramos and her beautiful daughter, Emma. They are seated here on the front row beside Mr. and Mrs. Kilpatrick.

"I met these two ladies on my way to begin my new job as you folks' pastor. Well, some unpleasant men had put on Mrs. Ramos and baby Emma. With some skills I have I was able to convince these men it would be in their best interest to go on their way and leave the care of these ladies to me. I believe God led me across their path.

"When you know someone cares for you and cares what happens to you, if you know they love you, it changes everything. Now you have something, someone to live for.

"Now here is a chapter and verse. Book of Romans, chapter eight, verses thirty-seven, thirty-eight, thirty-nine says, 'In all these things we are more than conquerors through him that loved us. For I am persuaded, that neither death, nor life, nor angels, nor principalities, nor powers, nor things present, nor things to come, nor height, nor depth, nor any other creature, shall be able to separate us from the love of God, which is in Christ Jesus our Lord.' Now this was my mother's Bible, and she had these verses underlined. Important to her, important to me.

"So here it is, folks, this life we live, live for the future, right the wrongs when possible, live peaceably with everyone when possible. The past is gone. God has a future full of hope for us.

"Now, folks, don't begin to believe that I don't know there will be pain and loss, perhaps some suffering in all of our futures, but now listen close, everyone."

At this point in the sermon, Mercedes noticed that Eli seemed to have a hard time speaking as before, with such practiced eloquence. Looking upward and tightly clenching his mother's Bible, taking a deep, labored breath his eyes began to water. There was total silence in the room. Slowly, the words begin to come back to him.

Eli

"There was a moment in time in my life when God, I am most sure, spoke to me. He said, 'My grace is sufficient for thee: for my strength is made perfect in weakness.' God spoke these words to my heart at a time of great loss. This loss I cannot speak of even now, with some years gone by, but to say God's grace is sufficient to give me strength to have hope for the future.

"Friends, forgive my emotion. As I look on this group of hardworking folk, know that I am glad to become a part of your town. If I can ever do anything for any of you, let me know. To end this service—I am not much of a singer, but perhaps some of you are—if we could end with the song Amazing Grace."

Seemingly as one, the congregation began to sing.

Amazing grace! How sweet the sound that saved a wretch like me!
I once was lost, but now am found, was blind, but now I see.

'Twas grace that taught my heart to fear, and grace my fears relieved:
How precious did that grace appear the hour I first believed!
Through many dangers, toils, and snares, I have already come:
'Tis grace hath bro't me safe thus far, and grace will lead me home.

Midway through the song, Pastor Eli walked through the congregation, singing, and placed himself at the door so he could shake hands with every man, woman, and child as they left the church, the dogs, Bill and Mary-Lou, sitting on either side of him and gladly accepting every pat on the head.

With every handshake of the womenfolk speaking for their family there was an invite to Sunday dinner, but Pastor Eli respectfully declined because he had already accepted the invitation for dinner with James and Sarah Kilpatrick. So with each invitation he assured each family he wanted to come and visit their home, and if the visit was at about suppertime so much the better.

Around the dinner table at the Kilpatricks', most of the talk was about the Sunday morning service and how fast people had gotten the news of a pastor in town, him only having arrived Saturday evening. "News travels fast in these hills," said Sarah.

"James, the barn and the living quarters are just fine. In fact, preaching in a barn I believe put me more at ease than if I had been preaching in a large ornate church building. But who owns the barn and won't they need it back?"

"Well, that is an interesting story, Eli. The owner of the barn has just recently told me we are welcome to use the barn as long as we need until we are able to build a proper church."

"Was the owner of the barn at church this morning?"

"Yes, she was, and she is sitting at this table now."

Both James and Sarah turned and looked at Mercedes, then with large smiles turned back to the confused face of Eli. Sarah said to Mercedes, "Tell him. He seems very confused." Then everyone at the table was laughing, even Emma, but not Eli, who wasn't really sure what was so funny.

"Okay. Elijah, remember when I told you that last year John came upriver scouting a town and some land to start a riverboat business? Well, Oakland was the town. Now I did not know until last night when you asked me if I knew a John Ramos, since he had the same last name as mine. Well, it seems my husband, John, had gone a little further with the business plans than I knew. He had met a man when he was in Oakland and hired him to cut the timber and build the barn for our steamboat business for a warehouse. The man he hired to build the barn, I believe, is some of your kinfolk, William O'Brian. So I say as full partner in business with my husband, the town of Oakland may use our barn until they can build a proper church."

The crack in the big man's voice was only slightly noticeable. "Well, I am always amazed at the hand of God, how where you go, he works things out and plans ahead, knowing the path ahead of us."

"Elijah, you took such care of me and Emma on the trail, saved our lives. I am so happy I can do anything that might be a blessing to you." Now the crack in the voice was Mercedes's and there was wetness in her eyes. Then suddenly Emma was laughing. Eli felt a movement under the table; looking under, he noticed Bill and Mary-Lou had somehow gotten into the house and were licking Emma's bare feet hanging down from the chair she was sitting in.

11

Monday evening at about 4:00 p.m. Eli, standing in the door of the barn, looked downriver, having heard a steam whistle. The boat was still quiet, some distance from the Oakland landing. About half the distance downriver to the boat was a slight bend in the river and a large bluff on the Oakland side. Eli estimated the distance to the bluff to be about a half mile, maybe less, and he remembered the water to be shallow under the bluff. The boat was approaching that part of the river on the opposite side.

There was a puff of smoke suddenly in the air above the bluff, a second later the sound of a rifle shot.

Looking closer at the bluff, Eli could see two men with rifles, the second shot now being fired. Quickly stepping back into his quarters, he grabbed his rifle; those men on that boat did not have a chance. Running through the front door of the barn, Henry in hand, he could tell from the sound of the rifles they were using single-shot, muzzle-loading guns, so this may give him an advantage with his Henry repeater fifteen-shot.

The men on the boat had taken cover behind the wheelhouse; the boat was getting closer to the bluff as they just could not stop. Eli ran to the large oak tree the church bell hung from. There was a large knot protruding from the tree, probably from a limb broken off many years before. The knot was just the right height for the Henry to rest on. Lifting the rear ladder sights and looking down the barrel, Eli estimated the distance to the bluff about seven hundred yards; the shot would be a miracle, but maybe he could get close enough to scare those men off. Firing his first shot, it fell short, hitting the water at the base of the bluff. Second shot landed on top of the bluff, sending rock fragments flying over the two men. One of the men ran from the bluff into the woods, but the other had reloaded and was ready to fire. The boat was close enough his shot would most certainly be deadly, so Eli knew this shot had to matter. Taking a deep breath, and after slightly adjusting his rear sights based on the placement of his last shot, he squeezed off his third round. The bullet from Eli's Henry struck the breach of the rifle just as the second man on the bluff squeezed his trigger. The gun exploded and went flying into the river; the man was sent rolling over the edge out of sight from the impact of the .44-40-caliber bullet.

"Thank you, Lord."

Rifle in hand, I walked down to the river shore as the boat drew closer to the bank, the young man on the bow looking familiar. When the front of the boat slid to a stop against the bank, John Paul Ramos jumped to the shore, extended his hand, and said as Eli took it,

"Mr. Johnson, sir, do you know where our mother and baby sister are?"

Eli was ready to take John Paul to his mother when suddenly they were surrounded by people from town wanting to know what the gunfire was about. Then there was a loud female voice heard above all others and something in the tone of the voice made everyone turn toward her. There behind the group of people stood Mercedes holding Emma. In a much quieter voice she said, "John Paul," and in a still quieter, small voice you could just hear Emma repeat her mother, "John Paul."

Running to John Paul, Mercedes threw one arm around him, squeezing Emma between them. John Paul took Emma from her arms just as Samuel and Emmett jumped from the boat and took turns bear-hugging their mother. In just a few moments, the bond between mother and sons was obvious to everyone. Then the look of joy turned to a look of question.

"John Paul, how could you possibly have known to come looking for us? I saw you and your father off. You would not have been back for three months. Samuel, Emmett, you boys left the day after for Texas. How, and if you are here, John Paul, where is your father?"

"Mr. Johnson, is there some place my brothers and I can talk to our mother in private?"

"Yes, John Paul, we will go up to the church."

When Emma saw Samuel, she wanted to go to him, so John Paul handed her off. Then when she saw Emmett, she wanted him to hold her, so Samuel passed her off. By the time they had walked up to the barn, Eli was holding her. There, he led them into the room to the left of the main room. Mercedes was tall for a woman, maybe five feet ten, but all of her boys were head and shoulders taller than her. The boys gathered close around her with John Paul taking the lead.

"Mother, our father was killed at sea. The two men who killed him were dealt with by the crew of his ship. Upon his death, I turned the ship around. When I found you gone, I was able to get in touch with Samuel and Emmett. They returned home, also, then we found your note, and Father's boat, the *Emma*, got us here.

Eli was watching Mercedes close as he listened to the news of Captain Ramos's death, her husband, his friend.

"In New Orleans, there were attempts to keep us from looking for you, and just downriver, Mr. Johnson saved us from two men who, it seems, were trying to harm, even kill us. A man I believe you know is behind Father's death, a Mr. Lithell Ewell. In fact, he is minus one eye, I believe, thanks to you."

Mercedes walked over to Eli, slowly reached out to Emma, and took her in her arms. Emma, sensing something was wrong, laid her head on her mother's shoulder and wrapped her arms around her neck. Mercedes sat down on the bench, tightly squeezing Emma to herself. Samuel sat on one side, Emmett on the other, both with an arm around her. John Paul knelt in front, laying one of his hands on Emma's back. His mother reached out and took hold firmly of his other hand.

Mercedes looked into the eyes of her oldest son who had seen his father die. Then she began to cry softly.

Eli knew then that nothing could be better for Mercedes than having this moment with her children around her. Her soft crying, mourning the loss of John, her husband; he would also mourn for a friend lost. During the time he had spent onboard with him, he had come to consider him a friend and a man to respect because of his love for his family and his love of God. After a while, Mercedes became quiet. Then she took a deep breath, slowly letting it out.

Looking up at Eli, she said, "Boys, this is Mr. Elijah Johnson. He saved our lives and brought us here. Your father knew him and John Paul knows him as he was a passenger onboard the *Mercedes* on the last trip from England. He was a soldier, now he is the pastor of this church, which your father had built for us to use as a warehouse. But I have told the townsfolk they can use the building until they build a proper church. Your father believed in God the way Mr. Johnson does, so I am very glad this building he had built is being used for a church where people will worship his God."

Each son came to Eli, shook his hand, thanking him for helping their mother and sister. And while still gripping their hand, Pastor Eli pulled them in close and spoke a word of encouragement to each of her sons.

There was a knock at the door. Eli answered it. It was the Kilpatricks and Sheriff Warren. "Mercedes, John Paul, Samuel, and Emmett," Eli said, "with your permission, I would like to step outside and tell the sheriff and the Kilpatricks the situation. Just to let you know, men, your mother and Emma have been staying with the Kilpatricks."

Outside, Eli explained the situation to Sarah and James, and then James introduced him to Sheriff Warren, who then asked about the shots fired.

"Sarah," said Eli, "I believe the family needs some time alone, but I do think that Mrs. Ramos will need you, if you don't mind."

"Of course, Pastor Eli, I'll give them some time before I go in."

"Sheriff, walk over to the bell tree, and if you look downriver you'll see that bluff just up from the bend in the river well. There were two men shooting at these men and their boat as they came around the bend. The shots you heard were me firing at the men on the bluff. I may have hit one of them. They seemed intent on killing the men onboard."

Standing by the bell tree and looking downriver, Sheriff Warren said, "Pastor Eli, I am very glad to have met you. If you can make a shot like that, I hope I am never in your sights. I will go down and see if there is any sign of these men. If those folks in there need anything from me, you just let me know."

Opening the door, Eli let Sarah step in first. As she stepped into the room, all three of Mercedes's sons stood. A mother is always proud when she notices how her sons treat another woman; giving her the respect she deserves is a way of giving their mother respect.

"Mercedes," said Sarah, "will you and Emma come to the house with me? In just a little while we will all sit down and eat supper. I am sure these men could use a good meal."

"Thank you, Sarah, we will. Boys, will you be okay?"

All three sons nodded their heads and together said, "Yes, ma'am."

As the week moved on, Mercedes would, early in the morning, walk down to the riverbank, go onboard the *Emma*, stir the coals in the stove, start a small fire, and make a pot of coffee for her sons and Clyde. Eli would walk down with his coffee once he saw they were up. Then after a cup or two, they would go up to the Kilpatricks' for breakfast.

By Sunday, everyone in town had met the boys, and all said how sorry they were to hear of John Ramos's death; most of the townsfolk had met him the previous year when he had visited their town, and all were quick to mention how pleasant a man he was and how much his sons reminded them of him.

Mercedes believed she needed to go to Newport and send a telegram to her lawyer, but she was worried that might let Lithell Ewell know where they were. Samuel and Emmett told her they would be very happy to build the steam up and take her to Newport.

John Paul told her how good the people of Newport had been to them, and he put Samuel and Emmett to blushing when he mentioned the sheriff's daughters, who had seemed overly friendly to them. John Paul poking at his brothers brought a smile to Mercedes's face, something Eli had not seen in a while. This came up around the supper table at the Kilpatricks', where Sheriff Warren was also a guest. Earlier, with Mercedes permission, Eli had told the sheriff of the events when he had first met Mercedes and the information John

Paul had learned of Mr. Ewell before they had left New Orleans to find their mother and sister.

"Mrs. Ramos, may I give you and your family some advice? This is based on what Eli here has told me, and from the point of view of a lawman."

"Please, Sheriff, I would like to hear your advice," said Mercedes.

"I believe the safest place for you and your family is here. Between myself, Pastor Eli, and his Henry. And there are a number of other good men in this town, all men who fought in the Civil War. Also, your sons. Anyone will have hell to pay if they tried to harm y'all on my watch. I need to go to Newport tomorrow. Those two men Pastor Eli shot at, one of them left some blood, so maybe he ended up in Newport looking for a doctor.

"There is an army colonel I have been working with. He investigates situations like this that are more than what a local sheriff can handle. I will also send him a telegram and ask if he may be able to inquire of the situation in New Orleans."

"Can this colonel be trusted?" asked John Paul.

"Sheriff," said Eli, "I believe I can answer John Paul's question. The man the sheriff has mentioned is Colonel William O'Brian. He is my first cousin. We grew up together, and I would trust him with my life. Our fathers were brothers. Until I was wounded in the war, we fought side by side. We have stayed in touch; in fact, he gave me that Henry rifle. The plan in our last correspondence was he would visit me in Oakland. He owns land in the town, just upriver, and his grandson built your barn we are using for the church."

"If you trust him, Mr. Johnson, we will also," said John Paul.

So early Monday morning, a week after the *Emma* had arrived in Oakland, the steam was up and her stern paddle wheel was pulling her away from the shore, heading downstream to Newport. Onboard were Samuel, Emmett, Clyde, and Sheriff Warren. John Paul decided to stay behind; Eli and Mercedes stood on the bank and watched until the boat was out of sight. Eli could tell Mercedes was worried for two of her children going away from her again.

"That Sheriff Warren is a good man," he told her. "In fact, I was told in a letter from my cousin, Colonel O'Brian, when he knew I was coming to Oakland that a friend of his was sheriff. He also told me Sheriff Warren had been awarded the Medal of Honor by President Lincoln himself."

"I see what you are doing, Elijah, thanks. I'm sure they will be back."

"Not sure what you mean, Mercedes," Eli said with a crooked grin. "Just giving you a few facts about our good sheriff. Also, I gave Emmett and Samuel my Remington pistols. You never know, they may need to shoot a snake in the river."

The two of them walked up to the church and seated themselves under the bell tree looking down at river going by. Both dogs lay on either side of Mercedes, nudging a little closer as she reached over and rubbed both of their backs; they could sense the sadness in her.

"It has always amazed me how dogs can sense emotions in a person and show love and a sense of caring, just the way God created them," Eli said. "They have been good friends to me, but these days I believe their loyalties have switched to you and Emma. If it is all right, Mercedes, I would like to tell you of the conversations I had with John on our voyage over."

"I would like that very much, Elijah."

"He spoke of his love of the sea and his love for you and of the children the two of you have. He was meticulous in describing the character and personality traits of each child and how one child seemed more like him and the other like you with a mix of the best of you both in each. He also spoke of your father, how much he respected him all the years he had served him, first as a cabin boy, eventually working his way up till your father offered him his first ship to be captain of. The story he told me—and his voice became quite emotional when he spoke—of the day your father offered him the ship, he said he told him he would accept the job of captain under two conditions. First, he would rename the ship the *Mercedes*, and second, if he could have his daughter's hand in marriage. John Ramos told me in those next few moments, which seemed like an eternity, your father, normally a very easygoing, always-ready-with-a-smile man, became very serious, and he, John, thought to himself, *I have either lost everything or I have gained everything.* Your father's face slowly began to show a smile, and with a choked voice, gave him his blessing. As he was shaking John's hand, he asked him, have you asked Mercedes yet? John told him he had. Then he said, well, what did she say? He told your father you said yes, but he should go ask her father, and if he said no then she already owned fifty percent of the ship and they would buy out his half and he might not get to see his grandchildren. This caused great laughter in your father, and he told John, I hope you know what you are letting yourself in for, may God Bless you both."

"Thank you, Elijah. John never told me all of that conversation with Father; he just said he had given us his blessing. In your sermon a week ago, you spoke of great loss, a loss that you have never spoken of with anyone. The pain I feel with the loss of my husband, I do not believe anyone could ever have felt this much pain."

"You should know I have prayed for you and your children that God would somehow ease your pain and give y'all a peace that is sometimes hard to understand but a peace within that comes from God. Know that I have prayed that prayer every day since we heard of the loss of John, and I will keep on praying. I will tell you of my loss with some reservations, which is this: I don't want my loss and the sadness you may see in me as I tell you in any way added to your own sadness."

"Okay, Elijah, I just need to hear from someone that life can go on; I need to have hope that I can still function and be a mother."

"With God's help, I know you can. Just as the war was beginning, I had been married to Mary for one year; she loved me in a way I can hardly understand. I know maybe you expect me to talk of my love for her and I did love her, but when I think of her I always remember the way she loved me. Her devotion to me almost made me feel guilty at times. When she told me she was going to have a child, my first thoughts, unlike some men, I suppose, wishing their firstborn to be a son, I hoped it would be a girl, and I hoped she looked like her mother. During the first of the war, I was not involved in the fighting. My duties fell to training men, so I was home a lot in the evenings. Let me tell you, that little girl did look like her mother. Ms. Bell, I called her, and Mary named her Annabelle. Those evenings, Ms. Bell was always in my lap or on my shoulders. Mary complained once that if I didn't quit carrying her so much she would never learn to walk.

"My first action was at Gettysburg. The fighting and loss of life was more than can be understood. The last day of the fight, I led a charge. The fighting was close hand at hand, many men by my own hand were killed, and then there was a burning fire in my chest. I have small bits of memory here and there of gunfire, the smell of gunpowder smoke, and being carried. Then it was night and looking up and seeing stars. Not sure how many days passed. I awoke in a bed in a room full of men, some of them screaming from the pain. The fever I had caused me to go in and out of consciousness. I remember calling Mary's name. The days turned to weeks, and I wondered, had anyone told Mary I was here.

"One morning when I awoke, Mary's mother was sitting beside my bed. She wore a small black hat and an all-black dress. The sadness in her eyes was not for me. Holding very tightly to my hands, she told me of the illness that took Mary. Then the screaming of pain was mine. Through the pain I asked her, what of Ms. Bell? She dropped her head and began to sob. Through the tears, she said the fever took them both to heaven.

"After she left, there were so many days of darkness. I don't remember how many. She came back almost every day to see me, but I could not speak. She finally realized seeing her reminded me of Mary and Ms. Bell. Then she did not come as often.

"The turning point for me came when my cousin William came to see me. He would pray with me when he came. He prayed for God's grace and peace to be in my spirit and that it would ease my pain. In those quiet moments at night when there was no sleep to be had, that peace and grace of God I began to feel. He, God, assured me with a knowing in my heart that if I walked the path he has laid before me, I will see them again someday."

"Thank you, Elijah, for telling me of your family. In my own pain I know that was hard to tell. I can't explain it, but just listening to you tell of your wife and daughter somehow eased my pain. I'm sure had I known them we would have been friends."

Tuesday evening, they heard the *Emma's* steam whistle as she came up the river. By the time the boat had reached the bank, most of the town had come down to meet it. The dogs began to bark as the boat drew close, so Eli laid down the Henry he had been cleaning and walked down to the dock. They had brought back two passengers: the sheriff's daughters. Listening in on the conversation as Emmett and Samuel were introducing them to their mother, apparently the girls were customers of the dressmaker in Oakland. The boys had offered to bring them upriver for measurements for some new dresses and then take them home the next day or the day after that.

Turning toward town, Eli saw Jeb and Ira Stockton and their five kids coming. Suddenly the two girls screamed like Indians and began to run toward them, and when they reached each other, the hugging began. Samuel explained that their dressmaker was also their aunt; the girls' momma is Ira's sister.

Sheriff Warren stepped off the boat and shook Eli's hand. "Pastor Eli, them two girls talked the whole trip, never a break, but the boys didn't seem to mind. They just sat there and listened to them. Good thing me and Clyde knew how to steer the boat, 'cause them boys was distracted. There was a telegram waiting for me in Newport from the colonel, your cousin, stating he and his men are on the way here and he has news for Mrs. Ramos and her children. He should be here in a few days."

"Thanks, Sheriff. Come on up to the church. I just made a pot of coffee."

Saturday evening, Elijah was sitting in the church getting ready for Sunday morning services, just letting God speak to him about what the message should be. There was suddenly the sound of horses riding up to the front of the church. Swinging open the two large barn doors, Eli found himself face-to-face with seven horses in a line, all mounted by heavily armed men. The big man in the middle spoke first.

"Elijah Johnson, I am here to speak with you about an incident that occurred over and just north of West Memphis. It was reported to us that a man and two dogs did bodily harm to twelve men."

The Henry never too far away had filled Eli's hand before he had even stepped outside. Bill and Mary-Lou had slipped around behind the horsemen and were giving a low steady growl, causing all but the big man in the middle to turn and look. The big man never took his eyes off Eli as he stepped down out of the saddle. Slowly, he removed his gloves and tucked them inside his belt. Then he took a step forward, which made the pitch of the dogs' growl go up a notch. He smiled and said, "Cousin Eli, would you call off your dogs and tell them we are friendly."

"Bill, Mary-Lou, come." Both dogs stopped growling, ran between the horses, and stood on either side of Eli.

"Men, dismount and say hello to some of my kinfolk. Next to myself maybe the strongest and best shot both sides of the Mississippi."

Once Eli stepped forward and shook hands with William, the dogs settled down from their protective way, even greeting each man as they dismounted.

"Where is a good place for us to make camp, Eli?"

"Just the other side of the bell tree there is a nice flat grassy spot overlooking the river, plenty of room to stake the horses. And in the stalls behind the church there is some hay and grain."

With a nod to his men, they started over that way with one of them taking the reins of William's horse.

"So, Eli, show me the barn that my grandson built and you folks are now using as a church."

"Well, step inside, William. This is the sanctuary, and over through those doors to the left are my living quarters and office. That grandson of yours is a master builder, almost like each piece of timber was chosen and hewed for its place and purpose in the building. As a matter of fact, my sermon for tomorrow is about purpose."

"I am glad my men and I will be here to hear it. What time does service begin?"

"Ten-thirty, cousin. I am glad to see you. It has been almost two years."

"You know, Pastor Elijah, I have never seen a church bell hanging in a tree."

"Well, it's temporary, till we get a proper church built, but I believe that tree as long as it stands now will always be called the bell tree. Y'all will hear the bell in the morning."

"Eli, if that Mrs. Ramos and her sons are around, I would like to speak with them privately, with you present also."

"Sure, William. I will go gather them and ask them to come to the church to meet with you. Give me a little time, as they are close."

When Mercedes entered the door to the meeting room in the barn, the colonel was seated, but he immediately stood straight, removed his hat, and covered the distance between them quickly, taking her hand only after she offered it, as is proper in polite society. She thought in that moment Elijah could just as well be his brother; the resemblance was remarkable, right down to the manners. She could tell there were some remarkable women in their raising.

"Mrs. Ramos, first let me say I am very sorry to hear of the loss of your husband. May I offer you a seat, ma'am?"

"Thank you, sir," she said as he held a chair for her. The sons entering the room with Eli behind them each shook hands with him and greeted him with a "Sir," then they all three stood around their mother.

"I do have some news for you from your home, New Orleans. It has been five months since you left. A Mr. Lithell Ewell has filed paperwork on your house and land holdings as abandoned properties."

This news caused Mercedes to stand quickly, the anger clear in her face and voice. This same anger could be seen on the faces of John Paul, Emmett, and Samuel. "Elijah, do you have the leather pouch I asked you to keep safe?"

"Yes, Mercedes, I will bring it to you." Leaving the room for a few moments, Eli returned and handed the pouch to Mercedes. She removed the contents and handed them to the colonel. He laid them on a table and carefully looked them over. "Now, Colonel," said Mercedes, "what do I need to do?"

"My advice, Mrs. Ramos, is for you to return to New Orleans with these documents and reclaim your property, also with your testimony, and if you will press charges we should have no problem putting Mr. Ewell away for a long time. There has been, for some time, an investigation into Mr. Ewell's business. The army has a few teams around the country such as me and my men who investigate reports of wrongdoing, land grabbing, and such. Some of these crimes go from state to state, so local sheriffs cannot touch them. The army investigator in New Orleans sent me a report that they know what he is up to but not any real proof. They have even discovered his investors are a group of lawyers who own a large part of New Orleans.

"Now, I cannot tell you what to do, Mrs. Ramos, but if you decide to go to New Orleans and press charges, my men and I will escort you and stay with you as long as you need us for protection."

"My sons and I have discussed this day. We want to start a new life here, all of us but John Paul, who as the captain of his father's ship wishes to return to the sea. Samuel and Emmett, I believe, are already forming attachments here. One person I am most concern about is Emma; Mr. Ewell has already made one attempt to kidnap her.

"It hurts me very much to think of being separated from her. I believe the safest place for her is here, though, but only if Elijah agrees to be her guardian. Will you, Eli, if I return to New Orleans?"

"Mercedes, I will protect her with my life as if she were my own daughter. I give you my word of honor as a soldier. With God's help and all of the strength within me, no harm will come to her."

The passion and strength in Elijah's voice put all in the room back for a moment, but especially Mercedes, who rose from her chair, took a step toward him, laid a hand on his arm, and they both for a moment just looked into each other's eyes.

Colonel O'Brian broke the silence in the room, saying, "Mrs. Ramos, if it helps to know, I will say of my cousin, Colonel Elijah Johnson, God help the man or men who ever try to harm Emma while she is under his watchful eye."

With her hand still on his arm and looking into Eli's eyes, she said, "I know, Colonel O'Brian. I have seen him in action."

12

"The title of my sermon this morning is 'Purpose,' with a subtitle of 'Where do I fit in?,' and as illustrations, I am going to use this barn we call our church, and also the tree out front we call the bell tree. When the acorn fell from the tree and perhaps was buried by a squirrel that never came back for it, the acorn sprouted into a sapling by God's design. You walk through the woods and see the sapling—would you think or could you imagine that someday the small sapling will grow to a size that, once cut and removed from the woods and formed by the hands of a woodsman, like William O'Brian, the grandson of Colonel O'Brian, could you believe the small sapling, as you all look up, could that sapling now be one of these huge beams that support the roof on God's church? Look around, folks, every plank and board in this building came from a tree, which by God's design came from a seed.

"My cousin William and his family are with us today. Welcome. Thanks for using what God provided to build this building that has become a place for us to come together and worship God. When I think of how God provides and purposes so many things and events in our lives … when I think back on those moments and events of my life that brought me to this moment … I do not know how it all could have happened except by God's hand of mercy and grace. When I look down where I am standing, then look up to him and realize he moves people and events with a divine providence, well, we will never understand."

As Pastor Elijah Johnson looked up he became silent, and quietness fell on the room. Them Emma, sitting in her mother's lap, spoke one of the few words in her vocabulary. With her hand stretched toward him she said, "Eli." The silence was broken as her mother tried to quiet her, but there was more than one laugh in the room, including a very loud one from the colonel. With a large smile, Elijah took a few steps to the front bench where they were sitting, held out his hands to her, and as he was one of her favorite people she jumped from her mother's lap into his large arms. Then, as Elijah had always noticed of her when he would hold her, she took possession of him. She would grab hold with both hands and hook her heels in, and she would look around as if to dare anyone to try and remove her from his arm until she was ready. Always, this was the way she would come into his arms; not so bad, he always thought.

"This child, although just beginning in life, God already has a purpose and future in mind for her. She is a blessing to her family now. It will be years before she will understand how God has provided a future for her or to come to understand his purpose for her life, but that does not keep her from being a blessing now. We all do not realize the complete purpose of our lives, not as God does, because he sees everything, but do not let the not knowing keep you from the doing. We don't decide God's plan for our lives—we discover it."

As Elijah handed Emma back to her mother, Mercedes was thinking to herself, this man of such strength and even capable of violence, how else could he have bested those twelve men who would have harmed herself and Emma? When he spoke these Sunday morning sermons there was such a gentle voice with a quickening that made you want to hear and remember every word. When he spoke of God, it was as one man would speak of another man who was a friend. *Why has God never seemed so real to me? My husband, John, also spoke of God in this way. I will speak to Eli about this before I leave tomorrow.*

"Let us think now of the tree out front, the one we all have come to call the bell tree. God provided the seed that fell from the tree that grew to a sapling that

grew to the mighty tree we now see. Now God provided the metal that was used to forge the bell that hangs
in the bell tree, and when the bell is rung we think of
God's church. I have been told by men and women
they can hear the bell for miles up and down the river
and all around our town, even into the valley and gul-
lies. These people, when they hear the bell, even if they
are not able to come to our church services the morning they hear it, have told me the sound puts them to
thinking of God and his blessings in their lives.

"So here is how God works. He moved on James
Kilpatrick's heart to purchase a bell in St. Louis, Mis-
souri, and have it shipped here before there was a church
or a pastor. Then James decided to hang it in the tree
in front of the barn provided by Captain Ramos, built
by my cousin William. God moves in mysterious ways,
amen. God knows what we need before we know what
we need.

"Here is a scripture for today. Old Testament book
of Isaiah, chapter twenty-two and verse twenty-three,

it reads: "And I will fasten him as a nail in a sure place; and he shall be for a glorious throne to his father's house."

"The verse says a nail driven in a sure place, that nail becomes a support, or the nail in just the right place will hold that something together. Just as you notice the placement of the support beams in this building, the builder had a purpose in mind when he placed each one there to support the other, then the building becomes a structure of strength.

"I hope you understand what I am saying today. If you do, then you each should realize how important you are to your families, how important you are to your town, and, at times, important to a total stranger. The friendship and love we receive from people in our lives is what makes life worth living. And with some pain related to it, even the love and friendship we had with someone no longer with us, the memory can make life worth living. There is the next friendship or person we may love or that may love us.

"I believe it would be good if we close this service today with a prayer for the ones among us who tomorrow will leave us for a while. Let us pray that God will protect them and bring them back to us."

The group of people in the church began to pray with a single purpose for the protection of Mercedes and John Paul and also for the colonel and his men. Mercedes was not sure why, but as they were praying she felt a peace for the first time since they had made the decision to go to New Orleans and face the problems there and, hardest of all, leave Emma. Mercedes noticed, as had become his way, Eli at the end of every service walked to the front doors of the church so he could shake hands and thank everyone for coming to the service.

After visiting with and shaking everyone's hand, man, woman, and child, Eli pulled the two large doors closed, and then turned and walked back into the church. On the front row all by herself sat Mercedes. When Eli walked around in front of her, he looked down as she looked up to him; her eyes were wet with tears.

"Mercedes, are you okay?" Eli said as he handed her his handkerchief.

"Eli, I am not, but you can help by showing me how to know God the way you do and the way my husband, John, did. You see, I have always been a good Catholic, going to mass every week, taking my children and confessing my sins to the priest. John never would go with me. He always said he preferred to talk to God himself. In the years we were married, I came to know that he did indeed know God personally. No man could be as true a man as he was without that relationship with God. His men on his ship and our sons respected him because of his fair but firm treatment of them. He spoke of God on such a personal level I never understood until I met you."

Eli walked to the side of the room and carried a chair, and set it in front of her. He sat down and held his hands out to her, palms up; she laid her hands in his.

"Mercedes, it is so simple I assumed you knew. The book of Ephesians in chapter two says, 'For by grace are ye saved through faith; and that not of yourselves: it is the gift of God.' Now here is the simple part, the book of Romans, chapter ten says that whosoever calls on the name of Jesus shall be saved. So you see, it really is just a matter of a simple prayer between you and God, and he promises in his word to know you personally."

Mercedes squeezed Eli's hands as she began to pray. "Lord Jesus, I don't know if I am doing this right, but I want to know you personally. Please hear my prayer, forgive me of my sins. I believe in you, Lord Jesus."

The room was quiet, the voices at the church picnic could be heard just outside. The colonel and his men had begun cooking a whole hog in the ground early Sunday morning and all the ladies had brought a covered dish; there would be more than enough food for everyone. Folks in the town just felt the best way to send Mercedes and John Paul off was with a big church picnic.

Mercedes slowly opened her eyes and Eli noticed the tears were gone. There was a large smile as she said, "Eli, I know Him."

13

Two weeks later, Eli stood on the shore holding Emma as she waved good-bye to her mother and brother onboard the *Trader*. Samuel and Emmett had made a run to Newport with the *Emma* to take the sisters home and brought back a telegram from the *Mercedes,* which stated they made it to New Orleans. The *Mercedes* had returned, was in dock, and they were staying onboard. The colonel and John Paul agreed she would be safer with the protection of the ship's crew around her. No sign of Lithell Ewell, who would make a court appearance in two days, September 15th.

After Samuel gave the telegram to Eli, he told him Emmett that he would be making regular runs to Newport; some of the farmers around could sell their harvest in Newport and would pay them to haul it onboard. Also, they could bring supplies back for store owners in Oakland.

"Boys, I have to wonder if these regular trips have anything to do with the sheriff's daughters."

With a bit of a grin Samuel said, "We are just businessmen trying to earn a living. And as for Anna and Isabelle, we may see them from time to time out of respect for their parents. Mrs. Hunt, the girls' mother, has given us a standing invitation to supper when we are in town. It would be bad manners not to accept, Pastor Eli. Also, there was a letter left for you at the telegraph office."

Staring at his name, *Elijah Johnson*, neatly written in a beautiful script on the envelope. Both boys knew he was wondering who would write him a letter. Emmett said, "That is Mother's handwriting."

Eli tucked the letter in his shirt pocket and said, "Well, men, I believe it is suppertime, and Mrs. Kilpatrick will not want us to be late. Let's go say hello to Emma. I'll read the letter later."

After supper and with a little playtime, Emma was ready for bed. Her routine since her mother had left was for Eli to take her to bed and tuck her in; he would leave the room, and after a few minutes, she would call his name until he came back in and said a prayer with her. The first night Mercedes was gone, Emma woke crying and very upset. Nothing Mrs. Kilpatrick did would calm her, so she sent James to get Eli. When he entered her room, she reached for him. A few minutes of Eli holding her, she fell asleep and did not wake till morning. So Mrs. Kilpatrick decided this would be the routine until her mother returned.

Sitting at his desk in his room at the back of the church, Eli opened the letter and began to read Mercedes words.

Eli,

    I write you these words in hope that I might in some small way tell you how much you mean to me and my family. Not just for saving my life and the life of Emma, but the time since John Paul told me of John dying, your words of comfort have eased the pain for all of us. The prayer you led me in Sunday has changed my life forever. This journey I must take is taking me away from a place I fled to out of fear but now is my home. Do not fear for me; your cousin William and his men never let me out of their sight. But I do almost feel you are here. The colonel and yourself are beyond a doubt cut from the same cloth. I also write this letter to let you know I left a bill of sale giving the barn and the land it sits on to the town for their church, and I talked to young William O'Brian Sunday about adding on to the church and changing the look of the structure to resemble a church building instead of a barn. He said he would begin working on it very soon. Also, he is going to build a steeple with a bell tower. He is such a wonderful young man with a lovely wife; he also is cut from the same cloth.

This next part of the letter is hard to write, because I am not completely sure how you may take what I have to say. So here it is: as I write this letter I am knowing that I will not see you for I am not sure how long, and I find that thought brings a certain sadness in me. I loved my husband, John, and that will never change, and by the way you spoke of your wife I know you loved her in a way that you can never love again. I suppose what I am saying is I want you to know I will miss you, and when I return I look forward to spending time with you.

Forever in your debt,

Mercedes

Eli read the letter twice. Her handwriting and especially her signature at the end of the letter were so beautifully written it reminded him of some of the handwritten books he had viewed in the museums of London. The last part of the letter was of some concern to him. He would and did miss her, but could he ever care for a woman in such a way that the loss of her ...? *Even in my mind I cannot finish the sentence. I will write her back.*

When Eli's cousin William had still been in town, Samuel and Emmett had asked him to help them mark trees to be cut for a proper boat dock and also as lumber for the additions to the barn; they had even marked some cedar trees for proper pews and maybe a pulpit.

Samuel, Emmett, and Eli, with broad ax over his shoulder, headed to the timber, Bill and Mary-Lou running ahead, the men's lunches and tools put on the back of the black horse (they would need him to skid the logs down to the river.

Swinging an ax always helped Eli think. Being from the city, the boys had not swung an ax that much, but they were strong and good hard workers, so Eli put them on the two-man saw. At the end of the first day, they had cut enough timber for the dock. Two of the largest logs they skidded down to the river. The next day, they would skid the rest down. Then they would set the post in the river and begin construction of the pier. Samuel and Emmett were ready to start their river shipping company by going farther upriver, but Mercedes had asked them to stay on the river between Oakland and Newport until she had their legal matters resolved. The work of building the dock kept the boys' minds off the sheriff's daughters, but maybe not, because they had a trip planned at the end of the week, and because of the trade business they were building between Oakland and Newport, as well as a few stops in between, the boys decided two trips a week were needed.

Eli thought to himself he might get to perform his first wedding if the courtships continued.

After a full week of cutting timber and skidding the logs down to the river, the posts for the dock were set in place. Monday, William was bringing over two wagonloads of rough-cut planks to lay as decking on the dock. Friday after work, Samuel told Eli they would leave for Newport at daylight and return Monday, and just to let him know, they would attend church there Sunday morning with the sheriff and his family. Eli told them he would have a letter for them to take.

After supper and putting Emma to bed, Eli walked back to his rooms at the back of the church. Mercedes was on his mind, as she had been all week.

Mercedes,

I pray when these words fall under your eyes you are well. Samuel and Emmett are happy with the progress we have made on the dock this week. William will be here Monday with the planks

Chapter 13

for the decking, so it should be finished next week.
Then we are going to start the remodeling of the
barn. I am very pleased with your decision to give
the land and building to the town for their church.
Emma is doing well since her mother is gone. The
job of putting her to sleep every night has fallen to
me. I don't mind the task so very much. She will,
I believe, someday have the strength and beauty her
mother has. I am teaching her to say her prayers
each night, and know she prays for Mom in each
prayer. I am with Jesus: he believed the prayer of
a child had the most faith in it because they have
not had a lifetime to learn doubt. Sounds like the
beginnings of a good sermon. I have missed you.
Know that, without the grace and healing of God,
I am a man with a past of violence, that the guilt
of it overwhelms me at times. I have never made
apology to any man for my actions but I feel you
should know the struggle that is within me. When
I think of you and your children, the time we have

spent in this town, there is a peace that comes over me. It is the same peace I had before the war, with my wife, Mary, and Ms. Bell. When you return, we will spend time together; the thought of no occasion for such saddens me. So come home soon. Bill and Mary-Lou also miss you.

Elijah Johnson

14

The courtroom was very hot, which added to the tense feeling in the room when Lithell Ewell entered with his lawyers and a few men who seemed uncomfortable to be there. Quickly, they found a place to sit at the back.

Lithell Ewell started to walk straight to Mercedes. She stood ready to face him, but suddenly there was a body between them.

"Good morning, Mr. Ewell. I believe I have not had the opportunity to meet you yet."

Looking around the man in front of him, Lithell, who wanted a few words with Mrs. Ramos before the court proceedings, noticed she stood with her son and a rather large group of weathered seamen around her. Now might not be the best time. Plus, the man shaking his hand had such a grip Lithell had to tighten his own to keep from having his hand crushed. Now the man was backing him up, so Lithell could not ignore or get around him but had to give him full attention.

"Who are you, sir?" said Lithell.

"I am William O'Brian, Mr. Ewell, and I will be representing Mrs. Ramos. Also, tomorrow morning I will be paying you a visit at your office."

"What will be the reason for your visit, Mr. O'Brian? Then I might be willing to make you an appointment."

"*Colonel* O'Brian, sir, and I have begun an investigation into your business. As a federal officer, I am appointed to look into unfair business dealings since the war. The federal government just wants to help the South get back on its feet economically."

Chapter 14

Before Mr. Ewell could respond, the court officer entered with a loud voice asking all to stand for the judge.

The lawyer for Mr. Ewell was very smooth—eloquence and many words without meaning. His portrayal of Lithell Ewell was one of a hardworking businessman who had the best interests of the community at heart.

William O'Brian presented Mrs. Ramos's case with just as much eloquence but also documentation to prove her ownership of the properties in question and a side note of threats made against her by Mr. Ewell, as well as the murder of Captain Ramos, which his lawyer objected to most loudly with many more eloquent, meaningless words until the judge finally shut him up.

The judge asked everyone to stay in the courtroom while he removed himself to his chambers to review the documents presented to him; then he would return with his decision.

Within thirty minutes, the judge returned to the courtroom. The court officer asked all to stand for the judge's ruling.

"Mrs. Ramos, I am sorry for the loss of your husband. Captain Ramos was a good man and a friend to me and many others. This documentation presented proves beyond any doubt your ownership of the properties in question, so I rule in your favor, and Mr. Ewell, I believe this court will see you very soon as a defendant. This court is dismissed."

When the judge's hammer came down, Mercedes could feel Lithell Ewell looking at her. She turned and faced him. He stared at her and then turned and looked toward the back of the room.

A shot fired in a small room is deafening and the smoke fills the room quickly. A second shot fired more smoke.

Mercedes found herself suddenly on the floor with John Paul in her arms.

Eli sank a blow of the ax in the large oak tree and did not pull it free; he suddenly felt a strong moving in his spirit to pray for Mercedes and John Paul.

Samuel and Emmett were cinching some chain around logs to be skidded down to the church. When they did not hear Pastor Eli's ax, they looked in his direction. He was on his knees with both hands in the air. His prayers could be heard as he prayed for protection and healing of their mother and brother. They both removed their hats, stood in silence, till after a few minutes he lowered his arms, stood, and took his ax in hand.

Colonel O'Brian looked down at Mercedes; she was holding John Paul, who had been shot. In her hand he noticed a small pistol he recognized to be the one he had given Elijah with the rest of the supplies in a box for him when he traveled from Memphis to Oakland. The small pistol barrel was smoking, still pointed toward the back of the courtroom where the first shot came from.

Elijah had asked William before they left Oakland to protect Mercedes, but he had also told him that those who wanted to harm her or hers might also need protection. He completely understood what Elijah meant. He followed the line of fire from the small pistol's barrel to the hole in the middle of the chest of the man sitting in a chair at the back of the courtroom holding a large smoking pistol, his head down and both arms draped on either side of the chair, dead.

"Colonel O'Brian, my son has been shot." The crew from the *Mercedes* had surrounded Mercedes and John Paul; Saul, who as well as being first mate onboard was also the ship's doctor, began to try to stop the bleeding. Saul told Mercedes he did not believe the wound was life-threatening but there was a bullet that needed to be removed; the men would carry him to the ship and he would send one of the men for a doctor who had experience with bullet wounds to meet them onboard.

As the smoke in the room cleared, Mercedes, with pistol still in hand, looked around the room for Lithell. He was gone. Of the men who had come in with him, one was dead, and the others were in hand by the colonel's men. Lithell's lawyer was still in the room but had nothing to say.

Three weeks since that day in court and still no sign of Mr. Ewell, but the colonel continued his investigation. He was headed now to meet with Mrs. Ramos and John Paul onboard the *Mercedes* to tell them of his findings. As he approached the boat, he was first met with a couple of seamen on the dock who were interested in why he was headed toward the ship. From the deck of the *Mercedes*, Saul had spotted him and called out to the men to let him onboard. Once on deck, there were other seamen who eyed him. Saul told the men, who had not been in the courtroom, who the colonel was, then the men went on about their business.

"A very protective lot, Saul."

"Yes, they are, Colonel, of their captain and his mother."

"I have come to speak with them, if I may."

"Sure. Follow me to the captain's quarters."

Upon entering, Mercedes came immediately to him, extending her hand with a smile. The colonel thought what a beautiful woman she was, and a very good shot. John Paul was in a large comfortable chair; he did not get up.

"Colonel, please do come in. We are very glad to see you," said John Paul. "Excuse me for not getting up. I am moving slowly these days and Mother eyes me when I move at all."

"John Paul, strong and young you are," said Mercedes, "but the doctor said even with the bullet removed it would take time with much rest for the wound to heal.

"Colonel, I hear that in the last few weeks you have been busy," said Mercedes.

"I have, Mrs. Ramos. That is the reason for my visit. I know that out of fear of another attempt on your lives, y'all have stayed on the ship with the protection of your crew. With information I found in Lithell Ewell's office, I was able to discover a group of men calling themselves an investment group who were the money behind him.

"The most important evidence was a record book he had kept noting specific amounts of money given him to take care of people. When reported dead or missing, this group would immediately lay claim to their lands and property. It was the same many times before with other people, as with your family. Elijah kept Lithell from a task given him by these men; these men are in jail with a list of charges that I believe will hold them until I am certain I have enough evidence for them to hang for their crimes of murder."

"What of Lithell Ewell?" asked John Paul.

"He has disappeared, but with the evidence I have there have been wanted posters printed and sent to lawmen all over. He will be a dangerous man when found and that information is on the posters."

"So, Colonel O'Brian, you still cannot assure me that he is not a threat to me or my family."

"No, ma'am, and that is why my men and I will be at your disposal when you decide to return to Oakland. Mr. Ewell's records show quite a lot of money he received for his services. I did not find any of this money, and he did not use banks, so I believe there are a few of his men with him as long as he can pay them. I do believe it is a matter of time before he is caught and brought to justice."

"John Paul has decided," said Mercedes, "in two weeks he will be well enough to set sail and resume his duties as captain of this ship. If he is well enough by then."

"I will be, Mother," said John Paul.

She looked at her oldest son with pride and a small smile; his father's determination was so evident in his eyes. "When he sets sail I will be ready to head home to Oakland, Colonel. I would very much enjoy the company of you and your men. Thank you for the offer."

She could hear the bell ringing before they rounded the bend. Looming above the tree line the new steeple was clearly in view as they rounded the bend.

The sadness was still in Mercedes heart as she recalled herself and Colonel O'Brian standing on the deck of the steamboat that would take them to Oakland, Arkansas, and as she watched the sails of the ship disappear over the horizon. Her oldest son, the captain; his father would be proud.

William O'Brian found Mercedes to be a very smart and lovely lady to talk to as they had many conversations on the trip up the Mississippi. But he noticed every conversation seemed to involve her asking him questions about his cousin Elijah Johnson.

But why had the church bell been ringing on a Saturday evening?

As the boat came closer to the new dock, Mercedes noticed a lone dark figure standing there; a man dressed in black holding a child. A little closer: the child was Emma. Closer the boat came to the dock, and Mercedes saw the eye patch.

Lithell and his men had been watching the town for a few days, being very careful to stay out of sight, learning the townsfolk's routines. The preacher was always at the same place every morning and always back in the evening, but he could be anywhere the rest of the day. With him and those dogs of his, he knew, it would be very hard to come upon without them a-knowing.

They had slipped into town on an evening when they knew most all of the men were gone, and Lithell's scouts downriver had told him the boat was coming.

His revenge would only be complete if Mercedes Ramos could see and know that he had taken her child. He lived every day with pain because of her.

The boat pulled up to the dock. Mercedes could hear Emma calling, "Mommy!" and reaching toward her. She also saw the hatred in Lithell's eye.

Eight men on horseback slowly rode up along either side of the dock, all well armed and each looking as rough as the next.

"Men, if anyone attempts to get off the boat, shoot them. Before we leave I will have a talk with the child's mother. Mercedes, I had plans for us. I had chosen you to be my wife. You would have wanted for nothing. Why couldn't you see that?"

With a crack in her voice, Mercedes said, "Mr. Ewell, please do not harm my child."

Where the dock met the shore there was a large cypress tree; Lithell's horse was tied there. He walked over to his horse, and as he placed Emma upon the saddle, a man stepped from behind the tree and slipped an arm around Lithell's throat and an arm behind his head. At his feet, Lithell felt movement and heard a low growling, more than one. There was a whisper in his ear; he was surprised. Not many men he had ever met were tall enough to reach around his throat, and there was strength in the arm at his neck.

"Mr. Ewell, release the child and I won't snap your neck."

Lithell's hand was on her back. He bunched her dress in his hand and yanked her from the back of the horse into the air.

The sight of Emma being thrown caused Elijah to release his grip, giving Lithell the chance he needed.

There was a scream from the boat; both dogs' heads went up, then together they moved under Emma and she fell on the dogs with a little laugh, jumping to her feet, thinking the dogs were playing with her. They both moved very close to her; any harm meant for Emma would come with a price.

All the action caused Lithell's men to turn and look in their direction. When they turned back toward the boat, every man onboard had a weapon aimed at them, including Mercedes.

Lithell, free from Elijah's grip, turned on him quickly, a pistol in one hand and a knife in the other. Without thinking, Elijah grabbed the arm with the pistol with both hands and spun around and threw his body against Lithell, throwing them both against his horse. The horse lunged back at them, knocking them both down. Both men came to their feet quickly. The pistol was gone, but Elijah felt a warm wet feeling in his side. Placing his hand there and looking at the knife in Lithell's hand, he knew he had been cut, but he had been cut before. Looking at him and crouched to strike, Lithell had a grin on his face. He came in low with the knife. Elijah was ready. The knife was in his right hand quickly. As he came in, Elijah reached down with his left hand, grabbing Lithell's wrist, and with his right landed a blow square on his chin. Thinking only of sinking the knife into Elijah, the blow was a surprise, setting him back on his heels spitting blood. Then the knife was in Elijah's hand. Looking down at his own blood on the knife he threw it over Lithell's head, causing him to duck; the knife landed in the river.

"I will kill you with my bare hands," said Lithell.

Elijah had felt the strength in the man when he had a hold on him and he saw the rage in his eye.

Both men began to circle. Lithell was very fast for a large man; the first blow Elijah blocked, but the second came quickly to the side of his head, causing a ringing in his ear, then a third blow took him in his side where the knife had cut. When he came in the third time, Elijah was ready. He hooked a foot behind his heel and shoved him hard, putting him in the dirt.

Lithell stood slowly, and Elijah saw Mercedes standing on the bow of the boat, her pistol pointed at him and the hammer back.

"No, Mercedes, I'm not done with him yet."

Lithell watched as Mercedes slowly laid the hammer down on the small pistol, but she kept it on him.

Bent over and holding his side with a look of pain on his face, Elijah knew that Lithell would come in very confident, with the same combination of blows most men he had fought. When they found a series of blows that worked for them, they were very predictable with their movements.

He took the blow to the body, being ready for it, but ducked the blow to the head. With his feet planted, he threw the punch with his right hand, striking just below the heart. The blow landed solid. With the stunned look in his eye and the sound of air suddenly coming from his lungs, Elijah knew this was the moment to finish. With both hands, he grabbed the lapels of Lithell's coat, shoving him back but not releasing him. Then he pulled him in quick and hard and struck with his knee the same spot he had landed the first blow. He felt and heard his ribs crack.

Releasing the hold, Lithell's limp body fell to the ground.

With a deep breath, Elijah stood straight as Emma and the dogs ran to him. She grabbed a hold of his leg and he laid a hand on her head.

"How's Emma?"

"Good, Eli, how's you?"

"I'm good, baby girl."

Epilogue

The Lord is good. So much can happen in a year. The sun was just coming up as Elijah Johnson, with Bill and Mary-Lou, was sitting under the bell tree, him having his first cup, looking down at the fog on the White River as it went by slowly. God got it right in this place.

This Sunday morning would be a different kind of service. He would—the thought of it causing a lump in his throat—be performing his first wedding, for Samuel Ramos and Anna Hunt, as well as for Emmett Ramos and Isabelle Hunt. All with the permission of their father and mother. Both girls were young, and both

Samuel and Emmett had treated them with respect as their mother taught them. But they were very nervous when they asked Sheriff Hunt for his daughters' hands in marriage.

What they did not know was Sheriff Hunt had told Eli on more than one occasion they were the kind of young men he and his wife had always wanted for their daughters.

Eli did not kill Lithell Ewell, nor did he let Mercedes; perhaps they would have been justified in doing so, but a killing one would always live with.

When Lithell's men saw him down and out, they gave up quickly. Colonel O'Brian had brought a warrant for the arrest of Lithell Ewell, so he and his men loaded them all on the boat and took them back to New Orleans to stand trial. It saddened Eli to know that the evidence against Lithell Ewell would send him to the gallows. Colonel O'Brian brought Lithell and his men into the church service Sunday morning after their capture, so Eli knew they all had heard of the saving power of Jesus Christ. Three of them prayed the sinner's prayer with him.

The dogs' ears suddenly came up and they looked toward town. Mercedes was heading their way with her coffee cup in hand. Both dogs ran toward her, circling her until she greeted them both and rubbed behind their ears.

Eli had brought the pot out with him, so he poured her a cup and refilled his own. She sat beside him, his arm slipped around her shoulders as if it always should be.

"Eli, you were right. We needed to let the boys get married first."

Order Information

To order additional copies of this book, please visit
www.redemption-press.com.
Also available on Amazon.com and BarnesandNoble.com
Or by calling toll free 1-844-2REDEEM.